THE BOY WHO WOKE THE SUN

THE BOY WHO WOKE THE SUN

A.T. WOODLEY
ILLUSTRATED BY MIKE DEAS

Red Deer Press

Published in Canada by Red Deer Press,
209 Wicksteed Avenue, Unit 51, Toronto, ON   M4G 0B1

Published in the United States by Red Deer Press,
60 Leo M Birmingham Pkwy, Ste 107, Brighton, MA 02135

Red Deer Press acknowledges with thanks the Canada Council for the Arts
and the Ontario Arts Council for their support of our publishing program.
We acknowledge the financial support of the Government of Canada through
the Canada Book Fund (CBF) for our publishing activities.

Library and Archives Canada Cataloguing in Publication
Title: Boy who woke the sun / written by A. T. Woodley ; illustrated by Mike Deas.
Names: Woodley, A. T., 1971- author. | Deas, Mike, 1982- illustrator.
Identifiers: Canadiana 2022041940X | ISBN 9780889956858 (softcover)
Classification: LCC PS8645.O63 B69 2023 | DDC jC813/.6—dc23

Publisher Cataloging-in-Publication Data (U.S.)
Names: Woodley, A. T., author. | Deas, Mike, 1982-, illustrator.
Title: The Boy Who Woke the Sun / by A. T. Woodley ; illustrated by Mike Deas.
Description: Toronto, Ontario : Red Deer Press, 2023.| Summary: "Eleven-year-old Elliot
is having a dismal pandemic summer when suddenly he's caught in the bubble of one of
his own dreams and transported to another world, controlled by evil butterflies, where
the sun doesn't shine. Along with his octopus sidekick, Elliot discovers the reason for
these butterflies-gone-wrong and realizes that things must be set right if he is ever to
find the way home. An epic middle-grade fantasy about discovering your true path."--
Provided by publisher
Identifiers: ISBN 978-0-88995-685-8 (paperback)
Subjects: LCSH Friendship — Juvenile fiction. | Environmental justice – Juvenile fiction.
| Coming of age – Juvenile fiction. | Fantasy fiction. | BISAC: JUVENILE FICTION /
Fantasy & Magic. | JUVENILE FICTION / Science & Nature / Environment.
Classification: LCC PZ7.1W663Bo |DDC 813.6 – dc23

Edited for the Press by Beverley Brenna
Design by Tanya Montini
The illustrations by Mike Deas were initially sketched on the computer
using Wacom Cintiq, then printed, traced onto thicker paper with brush and ink,
and shaded using black watercolour.

Printed in Canada

www.reddeerpress.com

For Jen

-A. T. W.

For Annie and Faye

-M. D.

ELLIOT

Larry was dead and the summer was off to a very bad start. Elliot sat on the edge of the rock, staring down at the little fish who lay motionless on top of the tidal pool.

"Oh, Larry," Elliot sighed. "Poor you."

Scooping him up in the palm of his hand, Elliot carried the fish down the beach to the water. He waded in up to his knees and placed him on the surface, watching as Larry drifted out to sea. Elliot was surprised by the sadness he felt, how big it was in relation to the little minnow who caused it. But then, Larry wasn't just a minnow. He was the closest thing Elliot had to a friend that summer.

It had been a difficult year. There was a pandemic going on, which meant everyone had to stay away from each other. Hands had to be washed, face masks worn, and everything had to be doused in sanitizers that smelled like cat pee.

Elliot, who'd just turned eleven a month ago, had learned a lot about the pandemic. He hadn't known that this disease could spread quickly around the world, and that it was easy to catch and hard to get rid of, especially for older people. He hadn't known something as small as a virus could shut down schools, camps, shops, restaurants, movie theatres, and stop people from seeing their friends. Their family, even.

He knew now.

Things were very different last summer, and not just because the pandemic had changed everything. Last summer, he and his sister Brooke played chess, and jumped on the trampoline, and laughed a lot. But then Brooke became a teenager and, apparently, that meant not being interested in anything having to do with him. Apparently, it meant only being interested in hair and Instagram, and how hair looked *on* Instagram.

At first, Elliot thought things had changed between them because of something he'd done, but his mother assured him that wasn't so. It was hormones, she explained, a teenage chemical that made hair grow, and moods swing, and eventually changed kids into grown-ups, all of which made Elliot think of werewolf movies. It also made him dread the day these hormones would come for him.

Elliot's mother spent her days glued to her laptop, working feverishly on terribly important things like spreadsheets and PowerPoints, liability waivers and rental forms, sometimes even taxes, which put her in a particularly bad mood. Elliot vowed never to do these things when he grew up. They caused only misery, as far as he could see. They stopped people from making eye contact with the ones they loved, and nothing should be more important than that.

Wading farther out into the water, Elliot swam to where he could dive down and touch the bottom, then let the air inside his lungs lift him back up again. Since he'd turned eleven, he'd been allowed to swim in the ocean by himself, so long as he kept in view of the house, which he always did. His house was on the edge of the Pacific Ocean, in a bay where there weren't any waves, which made it quite safe. Elliot loved the water. Often, he'd swim until his hands turned blue and his fingers got all wrinkly.

Last summer, his dad swam with him. This summer, Dad didn't swim with him at all. He was a busy man, always on the move from one exotic location to another, from Myanmar to Madrid, Shanghai to Houston, shaking hands with men in large hats. He didn't have the time. And Elliot understood this. Though sometimes he felt like he didn't have a father at all. Like he'd lost him somewhere along the way.

Even Elliot's little dog, Poncho, wasn't interested in him. Poncho stayed curled up on his mother's lap all day, listening to the sounds of her fingers *clickity-clack* on the keyboard. Maybe he found the sounds soothing. Or maybe he didn't like Elliot anymore. Maybe nobody did. Elliot wondered if he'd become radioactive. It certainly felt that way.

And so, Elliot spent most of his time down on the shore, watching the goings-on in the self-contained worlds of the tidal pools. He'd watch the crabs crawl around, the anemones and limpets grab at tiny food particles in the water, the chitons and sea hares—which were kinds of sea slugs—as they slowly made their way along the rocks. He knew all the species—most of them, anyway (nobody knew *all* the species). He'd learned about them from a book his grandfather gave him: *Citizens of the Sea*, which was like a bird-watching manual, only for the ocean.

But mostly he'd watch the tiny fish. Each had its own personality and unique set of quirks, and he named them all. There was Hubert, who was shy and reserved, preferring to poke around in the shadowy crevices of rock by himself all day. There was Mitch, a show-off, who swam around like he owned the place, puffing out his cheeks and intimidating the others. And then, of course, there was Larry, his favourite. Larry had a ponderous nature about him. He'd often stop and stare at Elliot, and they'd eyeball one another for minutes on end, the boy and the fish. Elliot could sense the thoughts inside the minnow's head, skipping from one idea to the next, like stones across the water. And he wondered what Larry made of him.

"What do you think, Larry?" he'd say. "Who am I?"

Larry, being a fish, could not answer. And in many

ways, Elliot couldn't, either. It was an interesting question—"Who am I?" He was a boy, of course. His name was Elliot and he lived with his mother and father, and sister and dog, in a house by the ocean. He went to school, had friends, liked fish. But ... what else? What truly mattered to him? What would he do with his life? What would he *be*? How does one even decide what they should be, anyway?

Now, Elliot dove down and touched the bottom, then floated back up, and when he broke through the surface, he recalled the final conversation he'd had with Larry the night before.

"I'm pretty sure I was a fish in another life," Elliot said, to which Larry puffed out his gills—a sign of agreement, Elliot thought. "Really?" he went on. "You think? What kind? A grouper? A barracuda? A guppy?" Larry puffed out his gills again. "*A guppy*," said Elliot. This surprised him. But when he thought about it, it made sense. Guppies were small but tough, able to adapt to just about any situation. Like Elliot, who had to adapt in his own way. Because Larry was dead, Elliot was alone, and the summer was off to a very bad start.

CROSSING OVER

Elliot swam back to shore and made his way out of the water, up the beach to the edge of his family's property. Night was falling. It was time for bed. He yawned as he opened the gate, then walked across the yard and went in through the sliding glass doors to the kitchen. His mother was sitting in front of her computer, as usual, next to his sister, who was glaring angrily at her phone.

"I'm going to bed," said Elliot.

"I'll be up in a minute," responded his mother, eyes fixated on her screen.

"*Urgh,*" blurted his sister, gripping the phone so tightly, Elliot feared it might break.

"Say good night to your brother," his mother said.

"Good night," said Brooke, sounding annoyed. She wasn't annoyed at him; Elliot knew that. She was annoyed at Instagram, or something she posted on Instagram, or someone else posted, or didn't.

"Good night," Elliot said, louder than he normally would. Then he went up the stairs to the bathroom, where he showered, brushed his teeth, drank a glass of water from the tap, moved down the hall to his bedroom, put on his pj's, and climbed into bed. He waited for his mother to come and tell him a bedtime story, although ... the odds of that actually happening were slim, as most nights, he'd be asleep before she got there.

Reaching out, he turned on *Nightly Meditations for Kids,* an audiobook his mother had given him when he started having trouble falling asleep. The book was read by a woman with a soothing voice. "Lie down and make yourself comfortable," she said, same as every night. "Relax and let go. Breathe in through your nose, and as you breathe out, let go any troubling thoughts or worries."

Elliot breathed in through his nose, but when it came to letting go any troubling thoughts or worries, he wasn't quite so successful. His worries had become more stubborn these days. It used to be they were about goblins hiding in his laundry basket, or stepping on tarantulas when he went to the bathroom in the middle of the night. But now they were about other things—*real* things he'd read or heard about on the news—and maybe that's why they were so stubborn: forests on fire, melting ice caps, an island of plastic the size of Russia, floating somewhere off the coast of Hawaii, growing larger every day. They kept him up at night. They made him feel powerless.

"Relax and let go. Relax ... and let go." She was persuasive, this woman.

Elliot peeked into the hall, but his mom wasn't on her way up, so he settled back into his pillow and tried to let go. And eventually he did. He slipped downstream on a river of sleep and into a dream.

The dream was about the ocean.

In it, he was treading water, all alone, in the middle of nowhere. It was dark and cold, and the moon was out. The stars were shining, and there wasn't a speck of land in sight, just water in every direction, as far as the eye could see.

Elliot called out, but no one answered. His heart

pounded inside his chest. He needed to get himself to safety—but how? If he were to swim and keep on swimming, he might bump into a castaway boat or a desert island. He might even be lucky enough to find his way home. It was worth a try.

So, Elliot put out one arm after the other and kicked his legs, but almost as soon as he started swimming, an object popped up in front of him that made him lurch back in surprise. It was white and oblong, with a red circle at one end. At first, he thought it was a strange fish with puckered lips, but then he realized it was actually a plastic bottle with a red cap: a detergent bottle. What was a detergent bottle doing in the middle of the ocean?

Suddenly, something else popped out of the water: a laundry basket. Then a tube. Then a suitcase. Then a toothbrush. Then a bag, then a package, then a container. Random objects were popping up all around him, plastic of every size and shape, coming together to form a crust on the surface.

That's when it dawned on him: *he was trapped inside the plastic island*—the one he'd read about! Elliot thrashed around, trying to swim his way free, but the debris kept blocking his path. A container bumped him in the eye; a bottle bonked him on the head; and his arm got tangled in a web of netting.

This was not a pleasant dream. In fact, it was turning into a nightmare, and it needed to end! Elliot was about to force himself awake, when something made him stop. There was a light in the distance, like a firefly hovering just above the water. But strangely, it seemed to be coming from somewhere else, someplace *other* than his dream.

He stared at the light for a while, mesmerized, until he noticed it was growing, expanding outward. A breeze touched the back of his neck. Elliot looked around, trying to figure out where it was coming from, but it wasn't coming from anywhere—it was *going* someplace. The breeze turned into a wind, rushing toward the ever-expanding light, as though the light was a window through which all the air was escaping.

And then, just like that, as though a spell had broken, Elliot woke up. Only he didn't wake up in his bed, staring at the early morning sun creeping in through the bedroom blinds; he woke up *still inside his dream*. One moment he'd been asleep, dreaming he was lost in the middle of a plastic island, the next he was awake, and yet *still* lost in that same plastic island.

How could this be?

Elliot knew he wasn't dreaming—he was sure of it, in fact. His head was clear, his senses acute, thoughts coherent. He could feel the cold of the water against his skin, taste the salt on his tongue, smell the brine in the air, just as he would in the real world. Only it wasn't the real world. It was a dream.

Wasn't it?

Elliot began to panic. He shook his head, trying to snap himself out of it. He even pinched himself, which really hurt. That's when he noticed the wind had died down and the light stopped growing. And there was a figure standing in the light—a dark figure, a man.

"Who are you?" Elliot said, frightened by the sight.

But the man gave no reply. He simply knelt down and stretched out his arm, offering Elliot his hand.

SPHERES

Elliot remembered falling asleep. He remembered lying in bed, listening to the meditation lady as he drifted off. He remembered dreaming he was treading water in the middle of the plastic island, and the light appearing, and all the air rushing away. He remembered waking up inside his dream and seeing the dark figure in the light. And now here he was, staring at the silhouette of the man kneeling down and offering his hand.

"What's going on? Where am I? What is this?" Elliot said, his voice shaking with fear. But the man gave no reply.

Elliot needed to think fast. He had only a few options, and none of them were good: he could either turn and swim away; stay put and do nothing; or take his chances and swim toward the man. The ocean went off in all directions, with no end in sight. If he were to swim away, he might end up more lost than he already was—so that wasn't a good idea. Doing nothing wasn't a good idea, either, as finding yourself face-to-face with a possible rescuer wasn't exactly the kind of situation that called for inaction.

Which left swimming toward the man.

The man was surrounded by an area of light that appeared to be an opening of some kind—like a hole in the sky—and when Elliot squinted, he could see glowing objects off in the distance. Maybe it was a way out.

At least the man *looked* like he wanted to help.

Elliot decided this was his best (least worst) option. So, he gathered his courage, took a deep breath, and started swimming through the plastic garbage toward the man. "You'd better be nice!" he shouted, which was a funny thing to say, but at that point, he couldn't have cared less how he sounded.

The closer he got, the more details he could make out. The man was big and muscular, with a body like a gorilla's. He was dressed all in black, with black boots, black gloves, and a black mask that covered his face.

The mask was smooth and reflective, without openings for eyes or a mouth, just a solid black surface.

When Elliot got to within a few feet, he stopped. The man was even more intimidating close up. "Who are you?" Elliot asked, but again the man didn't answer.

Elliot started having second thoughts. Maybe he should swim away. Glancing back, he saw the endless dark of the ocean stretching out behind him. He'd surely drown before he made it to land, if there even *was* land in that direction. He looked back at the man. Elliot had no choice. His heart beat faster and, swallowing his fear, he swam forward, extending his hand. As soon as he was within arm's reach, the man grabbed him, lifted him up, out of the water, and through the opening he was kneeling in. And when they were on the other side, it was as if one moment, he was in a world he knew, and then he was somewhere else, on the other side of where he used to be.

And what Elliot saw on this side was astonishing.

There were thousands of glowing spheres floating in the air all around them—above, below, ahead, behind— everywhere. Some were as small as grapefruits, others as big as hot air balloons. It was like an ocean of infinite moons.

Elliot gasped. It was overwhelming. *"What is this place?"* He looked back over his shoulder and saw an enormous sphere floating right behind them, with an opening in it—the very same opening Elliot had just passed through moments ago. And inside that sphere was his dream. It was still there: the ocean, the plastic, the moon, the stars, all of it.

His dream, apparently, was housed inside a giant, glowing ball floating in space—a dream sphere he'd just left.

Elliot looked down. Both he and the man were standing on the back of a small white cloud. The man bent down and picked up a set of reins. Was he going to fly them somewhere?

Elliot felt like he was about to faint. It was all too much. Looking back at the opening, he calculated the distance. It was roughly the same as the distance between his porch and his sandbox, which he used to jump all the time when he was little. He could make it. If he didn't, however, there'd be no telling how far he'd fall. There were countless dream spheres below him, as far as he could see.

The man pulled back on the reins, and the cloud lurched forward like a fluffy horse and chariot. It was now or never.

Elliot jumped.

FALLING

He made it! Elliot jumped back through the opening and into his dream, landing in the water with a splash. As he scrambled through the bottles and containers, the cartons and cutlery, he had no idea where he was going. He only hoped that if he kept swimming, he might end up back where he started: in his room, in his house with his family, where he belonged.

Glancing back, he saw the man standing on the edge of the opening, looking like he wanted to chase after him, but reluctant to enter the sphere for some reason. Why? Was it dangerous, somehow?

Elliot spurred himself on. "Faster ... *faster,*" he huffed, but the plastic debris kept getting in his way and slowing him down. He looked back again, and this time the man was standing even taller on the edge.

Was the man getting ready to dive through the opening?

Swim. Just swim, Elliot thought. Then he heard a splash and, sure enough, the man was in the water, swimming after him. And he was fast. Easily twice as fast as Elliot. It wouldn't be long before he caught up.

Elliot slashed his arms and kicked his legs, but as he did, a sound rose up all around him. It was a rumbling, like the coming of an earthquake. The water became turbulent, and waves appeared. The ocean started rocking back and forth, tossing Elliot around like a ship on a stormy sea. Everything was shaking, even the sky.

Elliot cried out for his mother, but did she even know where he was? He tried desperately to keep himself afloat, but he kept dipping under, taking in mouthfuls of water. And then suddenly, as if out of nowhere, the man was upon him. He reached out to grab Elliot, but instead, a deafening noise rang out—

BWONG!

The whole world lurched. Elliot and the man were thrown forward through the water.

BWONG!

The noise rang out again, followed by another lurch. And yet again, *BWONG!* It felt like the other dream-spheres were colliding with his own. *BWONG! BWONG! BWONG!* Three impacts in a row, in rapid succession, and then a final impact, which was the loudest of all.

BWONNG!

And with that, Elliot's dream-sphere broke apart. In an explosion of glowing bubbles, it splintered into hundreds of smaller pieces—orbs. Each orb held a part of Elliot's dream, and in one orb sat Elliot himself, in a pool of ocean water and plastic up to his waist. He was trapped inside a glowing bubble not much bigger than he was, and it was falling, along with all the others, drifting slowly downward.

To where?

Cautiously, he reached out and placed his hand against the wall. It was soft and smooth and warm to the touch, and when he pressed against it, he felt it give a little. He wondered if he should tear it open—but no. The orb was falling; it was probably the only thing keeping him safe at the moment.

Elliot closed his eyes, trying to convince himself none of this was actually happening, that, as real as it seemed, he was only dreaming. Soon he would be awake, and everything would return to normal, and all of this would just fade away.

There was nothing to fear. Just remain calm. Any minute now.

Any minute.

Any. Minute. Now.

He opened his eyes, only to find himself still inside the orb, sitting in the ocean water and plastic.

Elliot had always prided himself on being adaptable, but even the most adaptable of adaptable creatures— even the toughest little guppy—would've had a hard time adapting to this. This was off the charts.

"Think, Elliot, *think,*" he said, but he hadn't any time for that, as the orb touched down and—*POP!*— suddenly disappeared.

Elliot was now sitting in a field surrounded by tall trees. It was night, and there were hundreds of glowing orbs falling from the sky all around him. He watched as they floated downward, and when they touched the ground, they, too, disappeared, leaving behind their contents in the grass: ocean water and plastic.

These were the other pieces of his dream, he realized.

The orbs didn't seem ominous or threatening. They were gentle and enchanting. Beautiful, even. They had a peaceful energy that helped put Elliot's mind at ease and slow his racing heart (a little, at least). And when the last orb touched down and disappeared, and its warm light disappeared along with it, the blue of the moon took over, bathing the forest in an otherworldly glow. The moonlight was brighter than Elliot was used to, and extremely blue. It seemed both dark and light at the same time.

Elliot looked up. There were millions of spheres moving across the heavens in slow-moving rivers of light. They looked small from where he was sitting now—like little pinpoints—not the huge, imposing objects he'd faced when he was standing on the cloud next to the man in black.

The man in black.

He'd almost forgotten about him. Could he have fallen from the sky, too? Could he be searching for him somewhere nearby, at this very moment? The answer to Elliot's questions came in the form of snapping twigs and crunching leaves. Someone was approaching.

Elliot panicked. He looked around for a place to hide. There was a bush nearby, and he quickly jumped behind it. Crouching down, he remained perfectly still, listening as the footsteps grew louder. He peered through the branches and, to his horror, saw a dark figure emerging from the trees, stepping into the weird, blue moonlight of the glade. It was the man in black, his masked face scanning this way and that, searching ... for him.

Elliot considered running for it, but if the man was anywhere near as fast on his feet as he was at swimming, Elliot wouldn't stand a chance. So he kept as still as he could, praying he wouldn't be found.

The dark figure walked directly toward the bush, as though he could sense Elliot was there.

Elliot closed his eyes, wishing it all away. *Make it stop. Please make it stop,* he repeated in his mind.

And then, miraculously ... the footsteps stopped.

Elliot waited, listening to the silence. And when he opened his eyes, the man was standing there, right in front of the bush, frozen in place. Only he wasn't looking at Elliot, he was glancing back over his shoulder. There was a sound rising up in the distance, like the buzz of an approaching aircraft. Something was coming.

What now?

Without warning, the man tore off toward the trees, running faster than Elliot had ever seen anyone run. He looked frightened. But what could possibly frighten a man like that? Elliot clamped his hands over his ears as the sound grew louder.

Suddenly, there was an explosion of leaves, as a winged creature burst forth from the trees. It flew across the glade so quickly, Elliot couldn't see what it was, only that it was dark and frightening, about the size of a falcon, with enormous, fast-moving wings. And almost as quickly as it appeared, it was gone again, off into the forest after the man.

The buzzing sound faded, and the world fell silent once again.

Elliot sat, far too frightened to move. The forest remained quiet. Eerily quiet. He heard no crickets chirping, no frogs croaking, not a single living creature.

After sitting for what seemed like hours, he realized that if he wanted to find his way home, he was going to have to get up and start moving. He couldn't sit there forever. So, Elliot took a deep breath, got up, brushed himself off, and walked out from behind the bush.

Standing in the open field, he took a look around, and decided it would be better to travel in the opposite direction of the man and the flying creature—that way he'd avoid running into them again. At least, he hoped.

Elliot walked until he reached the trees. They were tall and ancient, covered in moss and hanging vines. "You can do this," he told himself. And, channelling his inner guppy, he put one foot in front of the other, and entered the forest.

LOST

Elliot stepped quietly over sticks and twigs and dry leaves. If there were animals in this forest, or anything else for that matter, he didn't want them knowing he was there, especially if they were anything like the man in black or the winged creature. But as he made his way over fallen logs and tumbling brooks, across rocks and root systems, past wildflowers and alien-looking mushrooms, never once did he see a living creature. It was night, of course, and most animals would be curled up in the safety of their dens, but after walking for as long as he had (which might have been hours, hard to tell without a phone), he'd expect to have seen an owl or a bat, or the odd spider clinging to its web. But Elliot saw none of these things, and heard nothing, either, which made him feel like the only living soul in the world.

Where was he? What *was* this place?

Was it another planet? Another universe? Was he in the afterlife? Could the man in black have been death, and had Elliot escaped his clutches, only to find himself trapped in that in-between place—what did they call it? Purgatory? Could this be purgatory?

He thought back over the events that had led him to this point: he'd fallen asleep; had a dream; woken up *inside* that dream, been chased by the man in black, and then his dream broke apart and fell from the sky— taking him along with it. Now here he was, wandering through a moonlit wood. Did that mean he was no longer asleep in his room anymore? If his mother came in, would she find him not there? Or had he somehow split off from himself, and there were now two of him in two separate places?

It was too much to comprehend. He needed to stay calm. He needed to—

Elliot stopped.

There was something lying under the leaves of a fern up ahead. It didn't look like a rock or a stump, or anything like that. It looked like ... an animal. Elliot stomped his foot to see if it would move, but it didn't. So, he picked up a stick and started slowly walking toward it.

Reaching out, he carefully moved the stick against the fern, lifting one of the big leaves. And when he saw what lay beneath, he gasped. It was the carcass of a dead animal. He couldn't tell what kind—a gopher? A beaver? But it looked to have been there a while (it was mostly bones). And the most shocking thing about it was that its skull was missing. It had no head. Just a body.

Elliot shivered. He put the stick down and carried on, trying to put the disturbing image out of his mind. He needed to focus on the task at hand: finding his way home. "Concentrate," he told himself.

He continued on until he came to a clearing, where the moonlight poured in through the treetops, illuminating the ground. He stopped and looked around. There appeared to be a footpath cutting through the grass and leading off into the woods. He went over to inspect it. The dirt was tamped down and there was very little overgrowth. It appeared to be well travelled.

So, there *were* living creatures in the forest.

If he were to follow the path, would he run into them? Would he want to? Several metres along, he saw a blackberry bush. His stomach grumbled. He was hungry, and blackberries happened to be his favourite kind of berry. Elliot looked both ways, then cautiously stepped onto the path and made his way toward it.

When he got to the bush, he stopped and stared at the clusters of hanging berries. They were plump and juicy looking. Delicious. He desperately wanted to try one. But ... should he? What if they were dangerous? What if, in this world, they weren't even blackberries? What if they were poisonous? He decided to take a closer look. Reaching out, he picked a berry and carefully rolled it between his fingers. It felt soft and ripe. He put it to his nose. It smelled sweet and earthy. Tart. It certainly *seemed* like a blackberry.

Elliot's stomach grumbled again, this time louder. *All right,* he thought. *Just one.* But as he was about to pop it in his mouth, the bush rustled, and Elliot jumped back in surprise.

"What are you doing?" whispered a voice from the berry bush.

"Who's there?" said Elliot.

"Never mind that," said the voice. "Why are you out in the open, when there's a butterfly about?"

"A ... butterfly?" said Elliot. "What's wrong with butterflies?"

"What's wrong with ..." The voice trailed off in disbelief. "Wait a minute, are you not from here?"

"No," said Elliot.

"Oooh," said the voice, taking on a friendlier tone. "Are you from Earth?"

Earth! So he *wasn't* on Earth. Elliot was shocked to hear his fears confirmed. "Y-yes. Are ... we not on Earth?"

"Not the Earth I come from, I can tell you that."

"You're from Earth, too?" Elliot cried.

"Shh! Keep your voice down."

But Elliot could not. He had far too many questions. "What is this place? How did we get here? How do we get back? How—"

"Quiet!" the voice scolded. "You're going to get us killed."

That stopped Elliot cold. *Get them killed? By what?* He felt a wave of dread wash over him. In his quietest voice, he asked, "Do you mean ... by the butterflies?"

"Yes. Now, please," hissed the voice.

Elliot stayed silent. He stayed life-depends-on-it silent. And as he stood there, staring at the bush, he noticed something nestled in among the branches. It was wet and slimy, like a patch of grey flesh glistening in the moonlight. It sent a chill down his spine.

Who was he talking to?

"Okay," the voice whispered. "Sounds like the coast is clear."

"Are you going to come out?" asked Elliot.

"If you promise me something."

"What?"

The voice paused. "Promise you won't eat me."

"Promise I won't—" Elliot was taken aback. He hadn't expected to hear anything like that.

"Promise you won't eat me," the voice repeated, obviously not kidding.

"Why would I eat you?"

"Because I happen to know your kind view us as something of a delicacy."

It dawned on Elliot that he might not be talking to

a human being. "Okay," he said, trying to remain calm. "I promise I won't eat you."

The voice paused again. "Why should I believe you?"

"Because, I just wouldn't. I would never hurt another living thing."

"Prove it."

"Well, when I find a spider in the house, I take it outside and give it a nice place to live. When there's a bee in the pool, I scoop it up and let it dry off on my hand, even though it might sting me, which it never does. When I walk outside, I always look at the ground, to make sure I'm not stepping on ants or anything. Once, I saved a baby bird that fell out of its nest. I rescued a grouper trapped in a tidal pool, helped a hedgehog cross the street, called animal rescue about an injured deer, petitioned people to stop shooting gophers, joined a group for—"

"Okay," said the voice from the bush. "I believe you."

"You do?"

"Yes. I think. Just know I'm equipped to defend myself if need be."

"You won't need to. I promise," said Elliot.

After a moment of silence, the bush began to rustle, and something emerged that made Elliot step back in surprise. It was a tentacle, and it slid through the dirt like a winding worm. A second tentacle appeared, then a third, then a fourth, and then more, until there were eight tentacles in all, dragging behind them a gelatinous blob of goo. That's when Elliot realized what he was looking at.

"You're ... an octopus."

"Very good. If you'd said 'squid,' I would have turned around and crawled the other way." The creature was grey, with hints of orange and purple, and had striking cobalt eyes.

"But ... octopuses can't talk," said Elliot.

"I'm not talking. I don't have vocal chords, and I wouldn't know your language to begin with. You're reading my thoughts and I'm reading yours. Not all of them, mind you, just the ones we wish to communicate, it seems."

"Is this a dream?" said Elliot, certain now that it must be.

"Unfortunately not," said the octopus. "I don't know about humans, but when we octopuses dream, it's never

in a linear fashion. Moments skip ahead, creatures and places morph into other things, and nothing stays the same for long. But not here. Here, everything is consistent. This is real."

The octopus started weaving four of its tentacles together into a single, braided appendage.

"What are you doing?" said Elliot.

"Readying my legs," the creature replied, braiding its remaining four tentacles into a second "leg." Then it stood.

"You can *walk?*" said Elliot.

"Not very well," said the octopus, lifting one suction-cupped leg and placing it down in front of the other. "But it beats sliding on your belly over rocks and sticks. Whoop! There we go. Come on."

"Where?"

"To find our way home."

Elliot watched as the creature stumbled forward, its rubbery legs bouncing up and down, its gelatinous head flopping about. It was one of the strangest things he'd ever seen, like an internal organ walking around on two legs.

"Let's go," said the creature.

Should I actually follow a talking octopus into the woods? Elliot wondered. And after a moment of pondering, he concluded that, while it was certainly bizarre and daunting, it was still better than being alone.

BUTTERFLIES

"All this walking really chafes my tentacles," whispered the octopus, as it waddled along the moonlit path.

"I'd lend you my shoes but they're too big," Elliot whispered back. "How is it you can breathe? On land, I mean."

"Same way we're able to communicate, I'd imagine. Different universe, different set of rules."

"What's your name?"

"Octopuses don't have names. Not like humans. We have more of a description, and it tends to change over time."

"What's your description?"

"He Who Longs to Fly Like a Bird. What's yours?"

"Elliot. How long have you been here?"

"Ten days, I think. Hard to tell without any daylight."

"There's no daylight?"

"Not that I've seen."

"You mean, it's like this all the time? With the weird bright moonlight and shadows?"

"Yep."

Elliot remembered what the octopus had said about the butterflies, and how he'd almost got himself killed. "What do the butterflies do? Why are they so bad?"

"Oh." The octopus shuddered. "They're vile creatures, whose sole purpose is to make you feel so sad, you wish you'd never been born. I was hit by one and barely found the strength to carry on."

"You were *hit?*"

"They fly right into you, straight to your soul. Make you lie down and never want to get up again."

"That sounds terrible."

"It is, believe me. Which is why you must always listen for them, even when you're whispering, as we are now."

"What do they sound like?"

"They make a buzzing noise."

Elliot gasped. He'd heard a buzzing noise when he'd seen the flying creature. "I … I think I saw one!" he blurted out, forgetting to keep his voice down. "I saw a butterfly chase a man into the woods!"

"Quiet!" said the octopus, stopping in its tracks.

Elliot stopped, too, and his stomach sank, queasy at the thought he might have just endangered them both. They stood stock-still, listening to the silence of the forest. And after several heart-pounding seconds, there came a sound. It was faint at first, but growing in volume. *It was the sound of buzzing.* And not just one buzz, but many.

"Quickly! Cover yourself!" the octopus said, flinging its legs out, allowing its bulbous, water-sack body to hit the dirt. Its skin began to change colour, mimicking the ground around it. Elliot realized the creature was camouflaging itself, while throwing clumps of moss and leaves on its body for good measure.

Elliot followed suit, dropping to the ground and piling leaves on himself, covering up as best he could.

"Don't move!" whispered the octopus. "Don't even breathe."

Elliot lay still, holding his breath.

They came through the trees, a battalion of winged

insects, patrolling the forest for signs of life. Elliot could see them with his one exposed eye: butterflies of varying shapes and sizes, some as small as birds, others as big as Elliot himself. They were black with blood-red eyes, and on their backs were strapped the skulls of dead animals. They flew low to the ground, moving slowly, the largest coming so close, Elliot could feel the push of wind from its wings, and could see that many of the skulls on its back were human. As it moved above him, its dark belly passed mere inches from his face.

Elliot's lungs began to ache. He feared he might lose consciousness. He stole a quick breath—just enough to keep from passing out—then held it again and waited. And waited some more, feeling like he might be trapped beneath the dirt and leaves forever. But gradually the buzzing began to fade, and the butterflies moved on. And when the forest was silent once again, Elliot allowed himself to breathe fully. Then slowly—*very* slowly—he sat up. Leaves tumbled off his body. The octopus sat up, too, and they both looked at one another.

Elliot laughed, quickly clasping his hands over his mouth.

"What?" whispered the octopus.

"You have hair," said Elliot, pointing to a patch of fuzzy green moss on top of the mollusc's head.

The octopus shook it off. "Well, I'm glad *someone* can find humour in a near-death experience," it said, obviously not amused.

"I'm sorry," said Elliot, realizing this was no time for goofing around. "Should we wait a bit before we get up?"

The octopus said nothing. It just sat there, staring straight ahead like a statue.

Perplexed, Elliot said, "Are you okay? Octopus? Hello?"

But the octopus remained frozen. That's when Elliot noticed it was staring past him, over his shoulder ... at something. Fear coursed through Elliot's veins. He swallowed, then slowly turned his head and saw what it was looking at. There was a butterfly hovering in the trees about twenty metres away, staring straight at them.

With quiet intensity, the octopus whispered, "*Run.*"

They jumped to their feet and tore off through the forest, as the butterfly screeched its sounds of alarm. The other butterflies came quickly to its side. Elliot leapt over fallen logs and weaved around jutting branches, but the octopus, with its strange excuse for legs, struggled to keep pace. Elliot looked back and saw the octopus falling behind. The butterflies were closing in. The octopus wasn't going to make it—he really wasn't going to make it. So Elliot stopped, and (hoping he wouldn't regret it), ran back toward his friend and the butterflies. He quickly grabbed the octopus and slung him over his shoulders, wearing him like a backpack, as he vaulted over rocks and slid down embankments. The octopus barely weighed a thing and so didn't slow him down, but the butterflies were airborne, and that gave them the advantage. It wouldn't be long before the terrible things caught up.

Suddenly, Elliot felt a searing pain in his ankle—he had twisted it. His leg buckled and he stumbled, falling to the ground along with the octopus. And while he managed to get back up, he could now only hobble.

The butterflies were closing the gap.

"No! *No!*" cried the octopus.

Elliot braced himself for an impact that never came. The ground seemed to rise up around them, and Elliot felt himself falling, pulled along with the octopus, straight through the forest floor.

WILD RIDE

As the trap door slammed shut above them, Elliot realized they'd fallen into a tunnel—and they weren't alone. He counted four kids wearing hooded cloaks, camouflaged with leaves and vines. The kids' faces were covered in mud, making them look like parts of the forest had come to life.

"Are you all right?" said the oldest boy, appearing to be in his early teens.

"Y-yes," Elliot replied, still shaken. "What happened?"

"We saved your life, is what happened."

They seemed like regular kids. They weren't aliens or forest elves, or anything like that. As far as Elliot could tell, at least.

"We were out foraging," the boy said. "You were lucky you ran into us. I'm Ronan. This is Fretrey, Ashwin, and Q."

"I'm Elliot. This is ..."

"Octopus," said the octopus. "Thank you for saving us."

"You're free to return to the surface, but it'd be best if you came with us," said Ronan, as he turned and walked off into the tunnel. The other kids followed, extinguishing the torches on the wall as they went.

Elliot turned to the octopus. "What do you think?"

"Well, we're not going back out there, I can tell you that."

Elliot agreed. He could still hear the buzz of insect wings, just beyond the trap door. "Okay, let's go."

They followed the group into the tunnel. It was damp and cool and smelled of minerals. The path twisted and turned, and Elliot could see, embedded in the rock, shining purple crystals that glowed, even after the torches went out.

"What is this place?" he asked, catching up to the others.

"The Mythica Gem Mine," Ronan answered.

"No, I mean ... what is this *world*? We're from Earth."

"Oh," said Ronan, glancing back with a knowing look. "You're in Lappanthia."

"*Lappanthia*," Elliot repeated. "Is there any way for us to get back? To Earth?"

"You can ask Granny Yilba. I'll introduce you when we get to the underground kingdom," Ronan said.

Elliot looked over at the octopus—*the underground kingdom?*

They marched until they came to a drop-off, where the tunnel arced downward and no further torches lit the way. The children pulled knapsacks out from under their cloaks, and threw them into a rusty old mining cart that was sitting nearby. The cart was mounted on tracks that plunged steeply into the dark.

"They're not getting into that thing, are they?" said the octopus.

Sure enough, Ronan picked Q up and placed her in the cart.

"Yep. They're getting into that thing," the octopus answered himself.

"Don't worry, it's safe," said Ronan as he pulled a lever, releasing the cart toward the incline.

"Are you coming?" Elliot said to the octopus.

"I am not getting into that thing."

"Yes, you are," said Elliot, grabbing his friend by the tentacles and scrambling into the cart, just as it took off down the tracks.

They shot through the dark, wind in their hair, glowing crystals whizzing by. The octopus screamed loudly (sounding like a cross between a dental drill and a crying baby), as the cart barrelled down the rails, turning corners at breakneck speed. The tracks curved up, then down, then up again, passing through caverns where bats hung from stalactites, and waterfalls sprayed mist into the air. Elliot howled with delight, losing himself in the excitement of it all.

"This is amazing!" he screamed, having more fun than he'd had in a long while.

"No, it's not!" the octopus screamed back.

The cart rounded a corner and, up ahead, Elliot saw something truly terrifying come into view: a solid wall at the end of the tracks! They were going so fast, they wouldn't be able to slow down in time. They were going to crash!

"WE'RE GONNA DIE!" the octopus screamed. And then he fainted in Elliot's arms.

Elliot steeled himself, shutting his eyes and leaning forward to protect the octopus. But rather than crashing, the cart burst *through!* The wall was just a curtain of hanging vines.

They entered an enormous cave filled with hundreds of children, running, leaping, kicking balls, jumping ropes, and swinging from vines tied to the ceiling, hundreds of feet above. A waterslide built of old mining equipment looped from one end of the cave to the other, launching a queue of squealing children into a lagoon. A collective roar of joy filled the place.

Elliot couldn't believe his eyes. He nudged the octopus. "Wake up! You have to see this!"

The octopus came to. "Whuh ... where am I?"

"*Is that a cake shop?*" said Elliot, pointing to a room carved into the rock, where kids were busy baking cupcakes and brownies, placing them on a countertop for passersby to grab (some of whom rode scooters). Cinnamon and sweet butter filled the air, and everywhere you looked, there was rock climbing. It was pure magic.

The place filled him with a sense of wonder and, for a moment, Elliot forgot he was lost in another world far from home. For a moment all he knew was ... he was happy.

The cart came to a rolling stop. "Come on," said Ronan.

They hopped out and followed the boy through the crowds of scruffy-looking children, many of whom were wearing tattered clothes. Some were even wearing bedsheets and rags, and most looked like they hadn't combed their hair or brushed their teeth in a long time. Judging from the smell, many hadn't bathed in a while, either. Despite all appearances, however, they seemed cheerful. There wasn't a mope or scowl among them.

Elliot, the octopus, and Ronan entered a tunnel with rows of alcoves on either side. Each alcove had been transformed into a candlelit room with a different theme: the mud room, the slime room, the glitter room, the room of balls, the room of ruining things, and the ultimate room: the room of mud, slime, glitter, balls, *and* ruining things. It was like walking down a street where every shop was the greatest in the world.

The tunnel led to a secondary cave, wherein several campfires burned. Ronan stopped and pointed to a bouncy castle, where an old woman was jumping, surrounded by laughing children. "That's her," he said.

GRANNY YILBA

Her face looked like a dried-up apple doll, and she wore no shoes, but she was extremely nimble, and had no issues keeping up with the children.

"Granny! New recruits!" Ronan called out.

The old woman stopped bouncing and looked over, and even from afar, her eyes were piercing. She climbed down off the bouncy castle, walked up to them, and stood there with her hands on her hips, staring.

Elliot found himself wondering why she was the only adult in the place. Was she some kind of witch? Had they unwittingly wandered into her lair?

"Well, well," Granny Yilba said. "What the heck are you?"

"I'm an octopus," said the octopus.

"Not you, I meant the boy!" She slapped her knee

and burst out laughing. She laughed so hard, she started hacking and coughing, and Ronan had to pat her on the back to get her to stop. "I'm okay—I'm okay," she sputtered, taking a moment to catch her breath.

Elliot glanced over at the octopus. *Was she out of her mind? Just eccentric?*

"For goodness' sake, don't look so serious," she said. "We keep it light here. We have to." She turned and faced a gathering crowd, chanting, "Granny Yilba keeps it light! Granny Yilba kicks the night!"

And all the children cheered as the old woman launched into a series of karate moves, kicking her legs and thrusting her hands out, yelling, "Yaw! *YAW!*" She threw a kick so hard, she slipped and fell, but rather than landing with a thud, she rolled along and then popped up into a ridiculous attack stance, hollering, "Hiii-yaw!"

Elliot couldn't stop from laughing along with everyone else.

Granny Yilba adjusted her hair and her smock, then walked toward them, huffing and puffing. "So, where're you from?" she said.

"Earth," Elliot replied.

"I can tell," she said.

"You can?"

"Oh, sure. You've got that 'just woke up in the wrong world' look in your eyes. You hungry?"

"Yes," said Elliot, whose stomach hadn't stopped grumbling since he'd seen the blackberry bush.

"What do you like?" she asked.

"Anything, really."

The old woman turned to the octopus. "What about you, Squiddy?"

"I prefer a diet of whelks, bristle worms, and crustaceans."

Yilba raised her hand and snapped her fingers. "Two orders of chocolate pancakes with extra caramel sauce, *toot sweet!*" Several children scampered off as she turned back to Elliot. "How long were you out there?"

"I just arrived," Elliot said. He pointed to the octopus. "But he's been here longer."

"Ten days," said the octopus.

Granny Yilba raised an eyebrow. "Impressive."

"Yes, well," the octopus said, "we octopuses are very good at evading predators."

Elliot was about to ask how to get home, when the sound of panicked voices echoed through the cave. Granny Yilba looked over at the entrance with concern.

"Clementine's been hit!" someone shouted, as a group of children ran in, carrying a girl. They were dressed in camouflaged cloaks (back from a foraging trip, most likely), and the girl was completely limp. She appeared to be dead.

Elliot recoiled at the sight, watching in horror as they brought the girl over and laid her at Yilba's feet.

"Quiet!" Yilba commanded.

The cave fell instantly silent as Yilba knelt down and placed her ear against the girl's chest, listening intently. Yilba's eyes darted back and forth for a few moments. Then suddenly, the old woman bolted upright. "Quickly! Emergency pony ride!" she cried.

Ronan ran off, while Yilba held the girl's hand, whispering, "Stay with us, child. Do you hear me? Listen to the sound of my voice." She was gentle and tender. Everything about the old woman—every move, every expression—made it clear she cared deeply for this girl. Granny Yilba continued whispering until Ronan returned with a pony, leading the animal through the parting crowd.

"Coming through!" he shouted.

"Get her on that horse, now!" Yilba yelled. "And stick a lollipop in her mouth for good measure, toot sweet!"

The children mounted Clementine on the horse, and she sat hunched over in the saddle, barely able to support her own weight. Elliot looked at her more closely. Her eyes were haunting, filled with a pain so deep, he had to look away.

"Did anyone find any *haaay?*" said a voice with a southern drawl. Elliot realized it was the pony, speaking without moving its mouth. "Anyone find any haaay?" it repeated, but everyone was too distracted to pay attention.

"Get that lazy nag moving!" screamed Yilba.

Ronan led the pony in circles as everyone watched.

The cave fell silent again, but for the sounds of trotting hooves and a hundred beating hearts. Some held on to one another, while others prayed, but all of them, every single one, remained utterly focused on the girl.

"There's nothing in this world that girl loves more

than a pony ride," Yilba whispered to Elliot. "She'll come back. You'll see."

Elliot watched as the pony raised its gait to a canter, and Clementine flopped around in the saddle. *What was happening?* he wondered. *Was this a kind of ritual?*

Yilba gave him a nudge. "Look at her mouth. Do you see?"

The corner of the girl's mouth began to pucker, ever so slightly. Quiet murmurs moved through the crowd.

"Nets at the ready!" Yilba shouted.

Children with butterfly nets appeared, and the murmurs turned into excited chatter. Clementine's pucker became a twitch, then her twitch became a smile, then the colour started returning to her skin. She straightened her back, sitting upright in the saddle. Everyone was shouting now, and some were shielding their eyes. Something was about to happen. But what? Elliot felt dizzy with anticipation.

Then, all of a sudden, there was an explosion of light, and a black butterfly burst forth from the girl's chest! The sight nearly knocked Elliot off his feet, but the girl appeared unharmed. She had no marks or wounds, no blood; she appeared dazed and confused, but otherwise all right.

"Now!" screamed Yilba.

The children swiped their nets, and almost immediately, one of the girls caught the creature.

The crowd went wild! They cheered and jumped, hugging one another and hollering at the top of their lungs.

Elliot and the octopus were swept up in a procession that moved its way through the cavern like a parade. Clementine—now fully conscious, but still groggy—was carried like a queen, as the girl who caught the butterfly led the way to a towering iron door embedded in the rock. She slid the door's bolt aside, pulled the handle, and opened it, revealing a cage filled with butterflies flapping around in the dark. She threw hers in along with the others, slammed the door, locked it tight, and turned around to face the crowd, shouting, "*The dark is yours to fill with light!*"

To which everyone thrust their fists up and replied, "*AND WRAP THE WORLD IN ALL THAT'S BRIGHT!*"

Bongo drums began to play, as scores of children ran off to dance around the campfires. "Time to celebrate!"

yelled Granny Yilba, throwing her hands up and kicking her legs impossibly high, dancing off to join the others.

Elliot shook his head in disbelief. "This is unbelievable," he said.

But the octopus's attention was focused elsewhere. "I've always wanted to try that."

"Try what?"

"That," said the octopus, looking at the children.

"You mean ... dancing?"

"Yes. Dancing."

"You should try it, then."

"Oh, no. I don't think so," said the octopus apprehensively. "What if I get trampled?"

"You can do it right here. That's the great thing about dancing, you can do it anywhere."

After a moment of contemplation, the octopus started bouncing up and down to the beat.

"That's it. There you go," said Elliot.

The octopus jumped into the air and flung out his legs, landing on the ground and tossing his body from side to side. He flipped and flopped, shimmied and shook, wiggled and waggled, as children ran up to place adornments on his head: a feathered cap, a flowery wreath, a pair of wire-rimmed glasses. And that's when he really let himself go. The octopus twisted into pretzel shapes, bounced off the floor, caught himself in mid-air, and spun around in circles like an ice-skater. But his greatest move by far was a rubbery rendition of squat-thrusts. The octopus crouched down and jutted his bum out again and again, over and over, until Elliot laughed so hard, tears came streaming down his cheeks.

A girl ran up, carrying two plates of chocolate pancakes. "Here you go," she said.

"Thank you," said Elliot, wiping away his tears.

The girl took out a fork and cut into one of the pancakes, allowing piping hot, golden ooze to slowly make its way out. "The caramel's on the inside," she explained.

"Oh ... my ... goodness," said Elliot.

FIRESIDE CHAT

Elliot and the octopus lay by the fire, basking in the afterglow of caramel sauce. Firewood snapped and popped, lifting hot embers through the smoke, and casting flickering shadows across the cave wall.

The octopus was still wearing the glasses the children had given him while he was dancing. "I think I can see better in these," he said.

"You should keep them. They suit you," said Elliot.

"They do?"

Elliot nodded.

The octopus took the glasses off and examined the hinges, the wire rim, the curved bridge between the lenses. His tentacles were graceful and dainty. They moved with a gentle intelligence. "Thank you," he said, placing the glasses back on his face.

"For what?"

"For rescuing me from the butterflies. You saved my life."

Elliot shrugged. "That's what friends do."

The octopus paused. "Friends," he said quietly.

Elliot looked at the octopus the same way the octopus looked at his glasses, studying him. "You're not really from my world, are you?"

"Of course I am," said the octopus. "Why wouldn't I be?"

"Because you're so …"

"So what?"

"Smart."

"You don't think octopuses are smart?"

"Sure, but not like you. I mean, how do you know so much? Not even dolphins and chimpanzees know the kind of stuff you know, and they're higher on the scale of intelligence—second only to humans."

"*Scale of intelligence?*" said the octopus, clearly offended.

"We have this scale of intelligence that ranks—"

"I know," said the octopus. "We have one, too."

"You do?"

"Yes. Let me explain something." The octopus shifted positions, getting settled in. "We have nine brains—one in our head and one in each tentacle. Knowledge is sacred to us, as essential as food and water. We study obsessively, educate one another, and pass our cumulative knowledge on to future generations."

"Not according to scientists, you don't," said Elliot, finding his claims more than a little dubious.

"*Scientists,*" scoffed the octopus. "Pardon me for being blunt here, but your scientists are a bit of a joke."

"A joke?"

"I'm sorry, I realize that's insulting. I'll give you an example. Let's say one of your scientists is observing an octopus crawling along the ocean floor. What do they see? They see an animal hunting for prey or searching for a mate—and it may well be doing those things. But what they don't see is the vast web of communication going on. Octopuses are psychic creatures, you see. We speak nonverbally across vast distances, with numerous individuals at once. But your scientists don't see any of this, so they conclude it isn't happening. Humans observe the universe in terms of their own faculties, which are limited at best, and in doing so, only scratch the surface of what it is they're observing. The fact is, there's more happening on the underside of a clam shell than your scientists have discovered since the dawn of time, which is why you're actually twenty-eighth on the scale of intelligence, not first."

"*Twenty-eighth?*" said Elliot.

"Just behind the scallop."

"But ... scallops don't even have brains."

"Not in the traditional sense, but they're highly philosophical. I'll introduce you to one, someday. You'll be surprised."

"Wait. If octopuses are so smart, how come they don't have rockets or microchips, or anything like that?"

"Rockets and microchips aren't the measure of intelligence. Not to us. Can humans spin a spiderweb?"

"No."

"Does that make you less intelligent than the spider? We have a saying: Don't explain sonar to a dolphin. Which is something humans fail to grasp. You're simply unparalleled when it comes to ego. That's where you truly excel. No other species even comes close. You place yourselves high atop the pedestal, looking down upon everyone else, while simultaneously choking the air and filling the oceans full of garbage. Are you aware that if the oceans die, so too dies the planet?"

Elliot looked at the ground. "Yes."

"What species deliberately works to wipe itself out? Certainly not the most intelligent, wouldn't you say? Rockets and microchips aside."

It was true. Everything the octopus was saying. Humans were reckless and destructive, and Elliot felt ashamed. "I'm sorry," he said.

"Don't be sorry," said the octopus. "Just do something about it."

"But ... I'm just a kid. What can I do?"

"Kids can do a great many things. Kids can change the world if they try."

Change the world? Elliot wanted to believe this, but it seemed so far outside the realm of possibility. Especially considering all the problems the world was facing.

"I'm sorry. I don't want to give you the wrong impression. I like humans," the octopus said.

"You do?"

"Yes. Especially you. Whatever you do, don't lose hope. And don't give up before you even begin." The octopus burped. "Ugh."

"What's wrong?"

"Those pancakes. I feel like I swallowed a boulder."

"You should stick to whelks and bristle worms from now on," said Elliot.

"I will." *Frrrt.*

Elliot felt his mouth curl up. He'd never heard an octopus fart before, and this one was ... well ... pretty good at it.

They sat for a while, staring at the fire. Elliot's thoughts returned to that haunting image of the girl's eyes. "The girl on the horse. She looked so ... sad. What was it like?"

"What was what like?" asked the octopus.

"Being hit by a butterfly?"

"*Oh,*" said the octopus, his voice deepening. "Well, the one that hit me was smaller than the one that hit the girl, but even still, the pain was unbearable."

"What kind of pain?"

"Emotional," said the octopus. "It was the saddest

sad I've ever known. I could feel it swimming around, somewhere between my stomach and my second heart."

"You have a second heart?"

"I have three. And each was set aflame in agony."

"What did you do?"

"I ..." The octopus paused.

"What?"

"I, um ..." The creature became bashful. "I thought about ... trampolines."

"*Trampolines?*"

"I know it sounds strange, but from the first time I saw one on the shore, years ago, I fell in love. Not with trampolines so much as the freedom they represented. The girl who was jumping on it, her expression was so full of joy. Leaping into the sky made her so ... happy. It was magical. And from that day forth, trampolines just became a part of who I am."

"He Who Longs to Fly Like a Bird," said Elliot, recalling his name.

"That's right," said the octopus. "And so, as I lay in the dirt, sinking ever deeper into darkness, I happened to think about them, and as soon as I did, I noticed a speck of the pain recede. Just a speck. So, I thought about them some more and, sure enough, a glimmer of light crept in. That's when I realized, I had to think about them as much as possible. So, I did. I focused and concentrated, and eventually, I felt a great battle taking place inside of me, as though the butterfly was under attack."

"By what?"

"Happiness. I think. I'm not sure how long I lay there, but just as I was about to give up and slip away— *pow!* Out it came."

"Wow," said Elliot.

"Nasty, vile creatures. I pray you never experience them."

The light inside the cave had begun to fade. The children were putting out the torches.

"Where do you think all the adults went?" said Elliot.

"It was the butterflies," came a voice. Granny Yilba had sneaked up on them.

QUESTIONS

Yilba sat next to them, lowering herself to the ground with a grunt. "We were a village once," she said. "Until the butterflies drove us underground. They picked the adults off, one by one, until they were gone. Mostly it would happen while they were out foraging. Someone wouldn't be looking the right way, or listening well enough, and there'd be an ambush. One time, the beasties got in through the ventilation system and it was a massacre. Just a massacre. The men went first. I don't know why, but they seemed to succumb quicker than the women did."

"Why didn't they attack the kids?" Elliot asked.

"They did. They attack anything that moves. Have you seen the skulls on their backs?"

"Yes."

"Those are their trophies."

Elliot was puzzled. "Then why are all the kids still alive?"

"They're not." Yilba hung her head. "Not all of them. Some didn't make it." She sighed heavily. "But it seems, the younger you are, the easier it is to hold onto your happiness. Gives you a fighting chance."

"So, it *is* happiness that forces the butterflies out," said the octopus.

"Yes. That's why we keep it light, here—we have to. And when we catch the little devils, we lock them up in the hopes they change back."

"Change back into what?"

"Into regular butterflies," explained Yilba. "When the sun returns."

"What happened to the sun?" said Elliot.

"It stopped rising the day the boy was imprisoned." At Elliot's confusion, Yilba continued. "The boy who wakes the sun. He's not a regular boy, mind you, he's an Immortal. One who holds the warm weight of heaven in his hands."

"Why was he imprisoned?"

"Because a man named Handsome Ned wanted the world to suffer for reasons I won't go into. He used black magic to turn the butterflies evil."

"Black magic?"

Yilba nodded. "Something that was outlawed, and for good reason. It gives those who wield it the power to bend reality to their will. Only, it can't be controlled—not completely. More often than not, it controls the ones who think they're controlling it. Ned got his hands on some and made his butterflies. But sunlight changes them back, you see. So, if Ned was going to have his little demons plague the living at will, he was going to have to get rid of the sun first."

"By imprisoning the boy."

Yilba nodded.

"Can't anybody free him?"

She shook her head. "Immortals are untouchable. They can't be reached."

"But ... Ned reached him."

"No one knows how. And no one knows where he is, either." She stared off into the distance. "But he's out there. Somewhere."

Elliot went straight to the question he'd been waiting to ask: "Have others from Earth been here before?"

"Yes. Over the years."

"Did any of them find their way back?"

At this, Yilba paused. "It's ... possible."

Elliot's heart skipped a beat. That was not the answer he was hoping to hear. "But you don't know?"

Again she paused. "What I know is, some went off in search of a way, and most returned, unsuccessful. But others didn't return at all. It's my belief that those that didn't return succeeded in finding that way."

"Or died trying," said the octopus.

Elliot felt an overwhelming sense of panic. The thought of never finding his way home, or seeing his family again, made his entire body shake. Yilba put her hand on his shoulder. "There, there. It's all right," she said, reassuringly. "You'll find a way."

"H-how do you know?"

"Because I sense your determination, your strength."

"Are you all right?" asked the octopus.

"I ... don't know," replied Elliot, doing his best to convince himself that Yilba was speaking the truth.

The old woman stood up. "We have a petting zoo," she declared.

Elliot felt his breathing start to slow again. "Really?"

"Yes. Would you like an animal to snuggle with tonight?"

Was that even a question? "Yes, please," Elliot said.

"What kind? A bunny? Chinchilla? We have kittens."

"Do you have any dogs?"

"Of course. What kind?"

"A ... Pomeranian?"

She tapped her finger against her chin. "You know, I think we just might." Turning to the octopus, she said, "What about you, Squiddo?"

"I'm really not one for snuggling. And please don't call me Squiddo."

"To each his own." Granny Yilba walked away, passing a group of children dressed in camouflage and emptying sacks onto the ground. There were all sorts of random objects spilling out: socks, a doll, baking flour, a banjo, candles.

"Where do they get all that stuff?" said Elliot with a yawn.

But the octopus was already asleep and snoring away.

A snoring octopus, thought Elliot. Lying back, he turned to face the fire, eyelids quivering. He pictured his mom and sister, and wondered what they were doing in that moment, if they knew he was gone, and whether they were worried.

But it was too upsetting to think about it.

Elliot wasn't sure if a great deal of time had passed, or hardly any, when Yilba returned with a fluffball that looked like a fox but was actually a dog—a Pomeranian, just as he'd requested. It looked like Poncho, his own dog, which, of course, was why he'd asked for it. The dog wagged its tail, grinning goofily.

"Thank you," said Elliot, feeling his heart fill up with warmth.

"You're welcome," said Yilba.

Elliot reached out and took the animal. It felt, in that moment, as if he were holding a little piece of home in his arms. Then a jolt of energy coursed through his body, and suddenly the cave around him was gone.

THE VISION

Elliot was floating high above the clouds, next to a mountaintop with two peaks. It was shocking at first, confusing and frightening, but he quickly realized he wasn't *actually* there. Not physically, at least. He was only seeing it, like images playing out on a movie screen.

He did his best to stay calm as he took a look around. There were clouds below him, and glowing spheres in the sky above. The double peaks of the mountain looked like the horns of a giant beast, and there was a ship sailing through the clouds, engulfed in ruffling purple flames.

What *was* this? Was it a dream? Something else?

Elliot started moving toward the mountain—*being* moved, like a chess piece across a board. He came to stop in front of a large diagonal opening in the rock. It was dark and cavernous, and from somewhere deep inside, a voice whispered to him: "*Elliot ... Elliot ...*"

Then, suddenly, he was back by the fire, with Yilba and the octopus looking down at him in concern, the dog still in his arms.

"Are you all right?" said the octopus.

"I–I think so," said Elliot, staring up in confusion.

"You fell into a trance. What happened?"

"I ... was floating in the sky. There was a mountain with two peaks. They looked like horns. And a boat moving through the clouds. It was so strange, like it was being shown to me."

"Fantastic!" exclaimed the octopus. "You had a vision! Congratulations!"

"Uh, thanks? I guess?"

"We octopuses consider that to be a gift. Did you see anything else?"

"A ... an opening in the mountainside, near the top. A voice was coming from inside, saying my name."

"*Hm. Interesting,*" said the octopus.

"The ship was on fire," Elliot added.

Yilba tilted her head, looking carefully at Elliot. "You saw a burning ship?" she asked slowly.

"Yes. And the flames were purple."

At that, Yilba's face turned pale. She staggered a bit, as if knocked off balance.

"What's wrong?" Elliot asked.

Granny Yilba paused. Then, with great seriousness, she said, "There's something you need to see."

~~~

They followed her through the cavern. It was dark and quiet, as most of the children had gone to bed at that point. She led them to a rock wall on the far side, with a large hole bored into it.

"This way," she said.

They went in, following a narrow passage that curved and snaked its way to a small candlelit room. In it, a bed was tucked in the corner, next to a desk piled high with books. There were paintings on the wall of a quaint village: houses with thatched roofs and crooked chimneys, villagers posing with their children and farm animals, wishing wells, horse-drawn carriages. It looked very much like a fairy tale.

Yilba moved to the desk and took a book off the pile, then plunked it down on the bed and started flipping through. Elliot and the octopus joined her, watching as she landed on a page. And what was on that page made Elliot gasp in disbelief.

"That's it," he said. "That's the mountain."

There it was: a drawing of the very same mountain he'd seen in his vision, with its double peaks rising above the clouds.

"Mount Valkrius," Yilba said.

"But ... how could I see a mountain I didn't know existed?"

"You didn't see it," said the octopus. "You had a vision, remember?"

"But why?"

"I think ..." The octopus took a step forward. "The path has revealed itself to you."

"What path?"

"The path home," the octopus explained. "The mountain was beckoning you. It was calling your name. It must mean there's a gateway at the top, inside that opening you saw."

"Gateway?"

"Between our two worlds."

That all sounded too far-fetched. Elliot's vision—if indeed that's what it was—could have meant anything, or nothing at all. "What about the ship?" Elliot asked.

"Perhaps it's a symbol of our journey ahead," said the octopus. "A vessel to take us home."

Elliot turned to Yilba. "What about you? What do you think?" he asked.

Granny Yilba paused. "I think … anything is possible."

"What about the ship? Why do you think it was on fire?" he pressed.

Yilba shook her head and shrugged. But something in her eyes let Elliot know she wasn't being forthright. And when Elliot thought back to the way she'd reacted when he first mentioned the burning ship, he was sure she was hiding something.

Elliot moved to the middle of the room and started pacing back and forth, deep in thought. "How far is it to the mountain?" he asked.

Yilba flipped through the book, stopping on a page with a map. She pointed to a patch of green in the

BLUE KINGDOM

IMANTRA

HAMINIA

MT. VALKRIUS

N W E S

upper corner. "We're here. In the province of Imantra, in the Northern region of the Blue Kingdom." Then she moved her finger diagonally down the page, over forests and cities, across a desert and through a valley, arriving at the drawing of a mountain—*the* mountain: Mount Valkrius. "A ten-days' journey by foot," she said, tapping on it with her finger.

"*Ten days!*" Elliot said. "We'd never make it. Not with the butterflies out there."

"I lasted ten days," said the octopus.

"But you weren't walking around out in the open the whole time. Besides, how would we even get there? We don't know the way."

"What choice do we have?" said the octopus. "We have to at least try."

The thought of travelling through a dark and dangerous world by themselves was terrifying. And the odds they'd make it to the mountain were slim at best. And even if they did, there was no guarantee there'd be a gateway waiting for them at the top when they got there. It was just a hunch at this point. And who would risk their life on a hunch?

Elliot sat cross-legged on the floor, burying his head in his hands. He was frustrated and tired. He wanted to cry.

Yilba watched him for a while, then walked over to the painting of a young man with brown eyes and a tweed cap. She stood there, smiling at it bittersweetly. She lifted the painting off the wall, revealing a hidden nook in behind. There were knickknacks and keepsakes in it: jewellery, broaches, letters, and a large bottle of something. She took the bottle and sat on the edge of the bed, dusted it off, popped the cork, and took a swig.

"*Ahhh*," Yilba hissed, wiping her mouth with the back of her hand. "You'll make it."

Elliot looked at her in confusion. "What?"

"You'll make it to the mountaintop."

"Why?"

"Because," the old woman said with a grin, "Granny Yilba's gonna take ya."

GOODBYE

Elliot awoke to the sounds of children preparing for the day. Some were lighting torches, others assembling baking supplies, or untangling jump ropes, or hooking up climbing equipment, and, for a moment, he felt an urge to stay. The cave was safe. It offered companionship and food, even a petting zoo and a water slide. The journey ahead, on the other hand, was filled with danger and uncertainty.

But ...

If he were to stay, there'd be no chance of his ever seeing his mother or father again, or his sister, or his dog. There'd be no chance of returning home. And that was simply not an option. Which made his choice crystal clear. He had to go. As frightening as it was, he just had to go.

"Good morning," said a little voice. It was the Pomeranian, nuzzling its snout into Elliot's chest.

"Good morning," said Elliot.

"Tummy rub, please," said the dog, puffing out its chest.

Elliot rubbed the dog's belly. And as he looked around at the early-morning goings on, he felt a certain unease. Because, although it was morning, it was still dark, and would continue to be all day, and all night, and all the next day, and so on. The world was stuck in a perpetual state of night. And it felt wrong to Elliot's very core.

Frrrt. The octopus farted again, holding his belly and groaning. "Uuugh."

"How's your stomach?" said Elliot.

"Turbulent," said the mollusc, putting on his glasses. "I had the strangest dream. I was back home, swimming through my favourite kelp forest, when all of a sudden, the world went dark, and a swarm of giant pancakes descended upon me from above."

Elliot laughed.

Then something caught his attention. It was lying on the pile of objects the children had left behind the night before. He set down the dog and went over to take a look. It was a doll with scraggly hair and a missing eye. He picked it up and held it out for the octopus to see. "Look."

"Yes, very creepy," said the octopus.

"No," said Elliot, bringing it closer. "Look at its boots." The doll was wearing a pair of little cowboy boots.

"*Oooh,*" said the octopus, clearly getting it now.

"Try them on," said Elliot, removing the boots and handing them to his friend.

The octopus wove his tentacles together and slipped each leg into a boot. Then he stood up.

"What do you think?" said Elliot.

The octopus bobbed up and down. He took a step. Then another. Then several more.

"*Well?*" said Elliot.

"I ..." The octopus stopped ... "love them."

"Yes!" said Elliot, clasping his hands together. "There you go. No more chafing."

Granny Yilba approached, carrying three knapsacks (one extra-small for the octopus) and three camouflaging ponchos, covered in leaves, sticks, and moss. "Put these on," she said.

Elliot slipped one over his head. It was dirty. "Smells like wet dog," he said.

"Mine's itchy," said the octopus.

"Small price to pay for your lives," said Yilba.

A crowd of children was gathering. "*What's going on?*" they murmured. "*Is she leaving?*" "*She couldn't be leaving, could she?*" Whispers spread through the cave, until the entire tribe had assembled.

"*What's going on, Granny?*" they asked.

"All right, everyone, quiet down," said the old woman. "I know you're wondering what Granny Yilba's doing with a poncho and a knapsack, so I'll just come right out and say it. Granny Yilba's going on an adventure."

Gasps from the crowd. "*No!*" "*Why?*"

"*Let us come!*" they cried.

"Now, now children. As for the *whys* and *hows*, the *how* is on foot with these fine gentlemen by my side. The why is for Granny Yilba to know, and Granny Yilba only."

They cried out in disapproval, but the old woman waved them off. "You know Granny can handle herself in any situation. You know that in your hearts. All will be well and good, and I shall return in due course. Until then, I want you to remember something and remember it always. You are good and strong children, each and every one of you. Never let what lurks beyond those walls bring you down. Never let it fill your hearts with fear. Live your lives to the fullest." Her eyes welled with tears. "Be kind to one another. Be loving. And above all, be happy. If not for yourselves … then do it for Granny Yilba!"

She launched into her karate moves, chanting, "Granny Yilba keeps it light! Granny Yilba kicks the night!" and the children roared with laughter. It was the greatest send-off the old woman could have asked for. "That's the sound I live for!" she yelled. "Now off you go! Toot sweet!"

As the crowd dispersed, Yilba went to speak with Ronan. Elliot tried to listen in, but they were too far away. At one point, the boy dropped his head, and Yilba raised it back up again with her finger under his chin. The boy looked like he was holding back tears as she spoke. Yilba kissed him on the forehead, and with a final nod, turned and approached Elliot and the octopus.

"I'm ready," she said.

THE FOREST

They followed a path through the trees. The forest was bathed in the strange blue glow of the moonlight, which, over time, became disorienting. Was it day? Night? Neither? It muddled Elliot's mind.

Yilba led the way, with the octopus following close behind, and Elliot bringing up the rear. Yilba was wearing a funny-looking contraption strapped around her head—essentially a headband with two brass funnels stuck in her ears. She called them her "hearmuffs," a butterfly-early-warning system that allowed her to hear faraway sounds.

The octopus was wearing his glasses, his cowboy boots, and a poncho, which made him look like some sort of weird garden gnome traipsing through the woods.

Elliot did his best to ensure they weren't being

followed, looking back over his shoulder and up at the trees every now and then. He was in a constant state of high alert—they all were—because at any moment, a butterfly (or Handsome Ned, for that matter) could jump out from behind a tree, or pop up from behind a bush, and there wouldn't be a thing they could do about it. Elliot asked if they should have brought nets with them, but Yilba explained that butterflies often travel in packs, making it impossible to catch them all. Nets made it more difficult to hide, and hiding meant everything when you were out in the open. If you couldn't hide, you were done for.

Onward they pressed.

After a while, Elliot began to notice objects scattered about the forest floor, random items lying partially hidden beneath the ferns and underbrush. Most of them were common things: a podium, a grandfather clock, a fish tank; others were quite strange: a carousel horse with a human head, a bicycle with feathered wings, a teacup with doll eyes. None of them, however—common, strange, or otherwise—had any business being in the woods.

Where had they come from? How did they get here?

Elliot was pretty sure he knew. Looking up at the glowing lights in the sky, he asked (in his quietest voice), "Do all these things come from the spheres in the sky?"

"Yes," Yilba answered. "They're called illunas—the spheres—little moons. They're the souls of dreams whose dreamers lie asleep across the divide."

"I was inside one," Elliot said. "Inside an illuna when it broke apart and fell. Are they all filled with drea—"

Suddenly, Yilba stopped in her tracks, and Elliot and the octopus stopped behind her.

Elliot felt his heart race. "What is it?" he whispered.

"*Shh,*" she hushed, adjusting her hearmuffs, listening in each direction. They stood in silence, as Elliot's heart thumped wildly inside his chest. Then ...

Errrp.

Elliot and Yilba looked at the octopus.

"Sorry," the octopus said. "Those darn pancakes."

Elliot breathed a sigh of relief.

They started out again and, as they did, Yilba turned to Elliot and whispered, "If ever a butterfly finds its way into my soul, get me to the sound of children's laughter. That's what I live for."

Elliot nodded and, as they continued on, he wondered, if a butterfly got into his soul ... what would work for him?

They hiked and rested, then hiked some more, stopping by the side of a pond where lily pads and bulrushes grew. Elliot and Yilba soaked their feet in the cool water, while the octopus took a swim. Later, they opened their packs to find cookies, cupcakes, and macarons, as well as an assortment of snails and slugs for the octopus.

"Wonderful selection Yilba, thank you," said the mollusc.

At the bottom of his pack, Elliot saw a harness, ropes and some odd-looking bolts. "What's all this?" he asked.

"Climbing equipment," Yilba replied. Which made sense. They were headed to a mountain, after all.

They ate wild raspberries from a nearby bush, and when they were done, the octopus burped and Yilba took a nap. When she awoke, they set off again through the moonlight. At one point, it began to rain, so they took shelter inside a hollow tree. There, they sat in the cramped space for what seemed like hours, as the rain poured down outside.

"How about we sing an octopus swimming song?" the octopus said.

"Sure," said Elliot, more than happy to break up the boredom.

"Just sing quietly," Yilba reminded them.

"Okay. It goes like this. *Ooooh, the octopus swim in blue so blue, the octopus swim in blue, the octopus swim so true so true, the octopus swim so true.*"

Elliot joined in. "*Ooooh, the octopus swim in blue so blue, the octopus swim in blue, the octopus swim so true so true, the octopus swim so true.* Come on, Yilba."

"Sounds like a cow dying in the pasture," said the old woman.

The octopus continued. "*Ooooh, the octopus dodge their poo their poo, the octopus dodge their p—*"

"Wait, *what?*" said Elliot, stopping him. "What did you say?"

"The octopus swim in blue?"

"No, the other part."

"The octopus swim so true?"

"No."

"The octopus ... dodge their poo?"

"Yes!" Elliot started laughing.

"What's so funny?" said the octopus.

Elliot couldn't stop long enough to answer.

"Well, you would, too," said the octopus defensively. "Sometimes the current shifts, and if you don't get out of the way, poo can get all over you."

Which made Elliot laugh all the more.

"Okay, that's enough," said Yilba, shutting it down. "You're making too much noise."

When the rain stopped, they set out again, pressing deeper into the woods. Their feet made sloshing sounds in the mud, which, over time, became hypnotic—one foot after the other, *squish-squish-squish-squish-squish-squish,* all so lulling and meditative. It felt like listening to the relaxing lady in the audiobook his mother had given him, Elliot thought dreamily.

Eventually, they reached an escarpment, where steady streams of water slid down a cliff onto the path ahead, then sloshed down a steep slope into a ravine. Yilba walked up and inspected one of the muddy flows.

"Do you know what that is?" she said, pointing to the rushing brown water.

"A ... mudslide?" said Elliot.

She nodded. "Then ... you must know, the last one to the bottom of a mudslide is a rotten eggplant." Yilba jumped into the air and landed in the flow, whizzing down the slope and disappearing off into the trees.

"Shellen's beak! What is that woman doing?" cried the octopus.

Elliot approached the mudslide and glanced down the slope, assessing.

"You're not going to jump into that, are you?" said the octopus.

Elliot glanced over at him, raising an eyebrow. "See you at the bottom," he said, then jumped in and flew off down the hill, doing his best not to holler. He rushed past trees and bushes, and when he got to the bottom, he was launched over the riverbank and landed in the water with a *splash!*

Resurfacing, he saw Yilba nearby, holding onto an overhanging branch. Elliot swam to her and held on as well, just as the octopus came barrelling down the mudslide, screeching. The creature flew off the bank into the river, then popped back up, looking dazed.

"Are you okay?" Elliot said.

"Define okay," said the octopus.

"No broken bones?"

"No bones at all," said the invertebrate.

Yilba let go of the branch, allowing herself to drift downstream. Elliot did the same, and they all moved as a group, floating on the slow-moving current.

"Now, this is my kind of travelling," said the octopus.

Elliot stared up at the trees as he bobbed along. He could see the twinkling lights of the dream-spheres—the illunas—through the branches, and wondered if he might be staring at the dream of someone he knew. Might he be staring at the dream of his mother or father?

Might they be dreaming of him?

Yilba swam to the edge of the riverbank and climbed out. She stood with her hands on her hips, looking down at the ground. Elliot and the octopus joined her. A stone path led off into a shadowy tunnel of trees.

"Where does it go?" said Elliot.

"Follow me and find out," Yilba replied.

IMMORTALS

Elliot and the octopus followed Granny Yilba into the tunnel of trees. The deeper in they went, the darker it got. Elliot's eyes burned from trying to make them focus in the dim light. Where was she taking them? Elliot trusted Granny Yilba—mostly—but there was always that niggling sense of doubt. What was it she was hiding from them, and who was she, really? Was she taking them to the mountain, as promised? Or somewhere else?

A form came into view up ahead: a towering human figure hiding in the dark. Instinctively, Elliot turned to run, but then realized it wasn't a giant or an ogre. It was the statue of a woman.

He stopped and caught his breath.

"It's all right. She won't bite," said Yilba.

The statue had a long flowing dress and wild swirling

hair concealing its face. Another statue stood just beyond it, and another beyond that. There were ten in all, some human, some animal, and some combinations of both.

"Immortals," Yilba said, answering Elliot's question before he asked it.

He recalled her mentioning Immortals before. "You mean, like the boy who wakes the sun?"

"That's right. That's him over there," she said, pointing to the statue of a boy roughly Elliot's age.

Elliot walked along the row, staring up at them. They were powerful-looking and godlike: a bearded man in a turban; a girl holding a lightning bolt; a porpoise; a majestic bird; a half-man, half-insect with six arms and pincers for a mouth.

"Each has a job," Yilba explained. "Bringing the rain, changing the seasons, moving the air. There's plenty more. These are just the original ten."

When Elliot reached the final statue and saw who it was, his blood ran cold: a large, muscular man with arms as big as tree trunks, and a mask with no face.

The man in black!

Elliot's hand trembled as he pointed. "Wh-who is he?"

"Who, the big guy? That's Barassas, shepherd of dreams," said Yilba.

"That's ..." Elliot could barely get the words out. "That's him."

"Who?" said the octopus.

"The man who entered my dream."

"A man entered your dream?"

Elliot nodded. "Through an opening in the sphere. He pulled me through, but I got scared and swam away, back into the illuna, so he chased after me. Is he bad?"

"Barassas?" said Yilba. "No. He's an Immortal. Immortals aren't bad."

Elliot turned to the octopus. "Is that how you got here, too? Did he—Barassas—try to pull you through?"

"No," said the octopus. "I simply woke up in the grass, having no idea how I got here."

"You didn't see a light, or wake up inside your dream?"

"No."

"Do you remember your dream breaking apart, and getting trapped inside a piece as it fell?"

"Like I said, I just woke up and I was here."

Strange, thought Elliot.

Why had the octopus's experience been so different from his own?

"What you described, Elliot, it's ... unheard of," said Yilba, her voice troubled.

"What do you mean?"

She looked at him gravely. "Immortals never reveal themselves to us. It would upset the natural balance of things. Those that fall into this world do so by accident, they're not brought here by Immortals. That's simply never happened—it never *would* happen. Unless ..."

"What?"

"Unless it was under the most extraordinary of circumstances."

Elliot chuckled. "Like what? Saving the world?" he joked. But Yilba didn't seem to find that funny.

"Yes," she said, very seriously. "Like saving the world."

Elliot felt as if things were speeding up and slowing down at the same time. His mind spun in dizzying circles.

"A mysterious current has surrounded you, Elliot," said the octopus, "and it's taken us along for the ride."

THE CITY

When they emerged from the trees, they found themselves on the edge of an embankment, looking out across the rooftops of an old city. Victorian buildings and cast-iron lampposts lined the shadowy cobblestone streets. There were no lights on, no smoke rising from the chimneys; it was all just quiet and still—a ghost town covered in a blanket of eerie fog.

"What is this place?" Elliot asked.

"Haminia City," Yilba replied. "At least ... it used to be." She walked forward along the path.

"Are you sure it's safe?" said Elliot, finding it more than a little creepy.

"Is anywhere safe?" said the octopus.

Elliot looked nervously down at his friend. "Let's stick together."

They caught up to Yilba as she entered the city. The streets were deserted. Shattered glass lay on the ground, and the doors and windows of the buildings were boarded up, many with holes punched in them. Some were broken altogether. Signs of a struggle. Perhaps many.

A sinister odour hung in the air. Elliot couldn't place what it was, but it filled him with dread.

"I used to adore this place," Yilba said. "So vibrant. Look at it now."

Fragments of lived lives lay all around them, thought Elliot ... a woman's leather boot, a postcard, an empty wine bottle. Signs on storefronts read, "Hotel Haminia," "Music & Dancing," "Coffee." There had been life here once.

The street led to a square with an ornate fountain at its centre, and it was there they came across a disturbing sight, one Elliot wasn't quite prepared for: graves—rows of graves dug into the dirt, covering most, if not all, of the space. Some had headstones, others wooden boards with names on them, and some had no markings at all. A shiver ran down Elliot's spine. "Can ... can we go back to the path now?" he said quietly.

"Look here," said the octopus, standing next to a headstone with a freshly picked flower on it. "That flower was put there recently. By someone."

"Do you think there are still people here?" Elliot whispered.

"Shh," said Yilba.

Footsteps were approaching—heavy footsteps. The octopus slid under an overturned skillet on the ground, while Yilba grabbed Elliot and pulled him behind the fountain. They crouched down and listened as the footsteps grew louder. Elliot feared whoever—or whatever—was approaching, might have had something to do with all the death surrounding them.

Could it be Handsome Ned?

Yilba peered out from behind the fountain, and Elliot followed suit. What entered the square next was enormous. It was a man, ten feet tall and made entirely of metal. His head looked like an upside-down bucket, and his eyes like puncture holes. He was carrying a stone, lumbering up to a grave, and setting it down, just so.

Elliot couldn't believe his eyes—a real, live robot! Something touched his shoulder and he jumped with fright. It was Yilba.

"It's all right," she whispered. Then she stood up.

"Yilba!" said Elliot, trying to stop her. But it was too late. The machine man had seen her and stopped what it was doing.

Yilba walked toward the giant. "Is anyone else here?"

"No," the machine man replied, his voice fed through a broken speaker. "I am the last."

Her eyes scanned across the rows of graves. "What happened?"

"A series of butterfly attacks over time," said the machine.

Yilba shook her head. "And did you bury them all?"

"Yes. That is my final task. Task #871: provide proper burials for all remaining Haminian citizens."

"Who issued it?"

"My master, who is there." The machine man pointed to the grave with the freshly picked flower on it.

Realizing the giant posed no threat, Elliot stood. He had a question he wanted to ask. He walked over and waved his hand in greeting. "Hi, I'm Elliot. What's your name?"

The machine man turned his turret-like head. "I am task machine serial number TM920."

"Pleased to meet you, TM920. May I ask a question?"

"You may."

"Why did you say this is your final task?"

The machine man pointed to an indicator on his chest. "My fuel tank is running low. Soon it will be empty, and I will no longer function. Are you carrying bitonium fuel?"

"No," said Yilba.

"Do you know where I might acquire some?"

"I'm afraid not," she said.

The giant glanced at the ground. "I must complete task #871 before my fuel runs dry." Then he knelt to mark the headstone he'd laid, after which, he picked up another stone, and positioned it near the head of a different grave. Elliot watched the machine man go about his business. His movements were slow and heavy. Sad, even.

Yilba adjusted her hearmuffs.

"Did you hear something?" Elliot asked.

"Not sure," she replied, walking away to get a better listen.

The octopus crawled out from under the skillet to

join Elliot. "This place makes me nervous," he said. "We should go."

"Don't you think we should stay and help him?" said Elliot, motioning to the machine man.

"No."

"Why not? Don't you feel sorry for him?"

"You can't feel sorry for machines. They have no feelings."

Elliot shrugged. "Maybe this one does."

"It doesn't. If it did, it would be lying in a grave next to everyone else. The butterflies would have made sure of that by now. But it's not. Do you know why?"

"I'm pretty sure you're about to tell me," said Elliot.

"It hasn't any emotions for the butterflies to prey upon."

A good point, Elliot thought. But still, he couldn't help feeling there was more to this machine than cold, hard steel. And he knew how he could prove it. "May I ask another question?"

"You may," the machine man said.

"Who put the flower on your master's grave?"

The machine man paused. "I did."

"Was that part of your task?"

The machine man paused again. "No."

"Why did you do it, then?"

The machine man didn't answer.

"Come on, Elliot, let's go," said the octopus.

But Elliot persisted. "Did you feel you needed to, for some reason?"

Again, the machine man didn't answer. But his silence spoke volumes to Elliot. The machine man hadn't understood his own actions, only that he had to express his feelings somehow—feelings of sorrow and loss, not just for his master, but for all those he'd laid in the ground. And the only way he could do that was through a flower.

Elliot looked at the octopus and said, "That's it. We're helping him."

"Elliot, allow me to explain something," said the octopus. He was about to launch a rebuttal, when Yilba's voice came hollering from across the square:

"Hide! Now!"

They were coming.

THE ATTACK

Yilba ducked behind a building, and the octopus slid beneath the skillet again, but Elliot, who was standing in the middle of the square, had no good place to go. He was too far from the buildings, and his leaf-covered cloak wasn't going to give him cover in the middle of a city. His only chance was to climb into the basin of the fountain and lie perfectly still, which is exactly what he did, as quickly as possible.

They entered the square—a group of black butterflies with monstrous red eyes. They were larger than the ones Elliot had seen before. Several of them were the size of large dogs. And all had more than a few skulls tied to their backs (most of them human). They moved slowly and deliberately, fanning out in military formation, taking their time to respect every nook and cranny. Elliot knew it wouldn't be long before they had him in their sights. He only hoped that his playing dead might convince them he was just another body waiting for burial by the task machine. He held his breath and tried to clear all thoughts from his mind.

The demons made their way over the graves, then up above the fountain ... then they stopped. They hovered there, like a fleet of helicopters, sights trained on their target below. Elliot could feel their searing gaze upon him. *Keep moving. Keep moving,* he thought. But they stayed where they were, right above him, until a sound shot a bolt of terror straight through him—

Skreeeeeeeech!

Elliot jumped to his feet and vaulted over the rim of the fountain, landing on the ground with a thud. He ran faster than he'd ever run before, jumping over graves and weaving around headstones. But the butterflies flew after him, catching up almost instantly, one of them moving in so close, he could feel the brush of its antennae against the back of his neck.

He wasn't going to make it. He was going to be hit. Elliot screamed.

Then, suddenly, he fell to the ground, pushed by a massive weight that bore down on him, pressing him into the dirt. It was the machine man, forming a shield around the boy. The butterflies crashed into the metal, slamming again and again—*Bang! Bang! Bangbang-bang! Bang!*—like a hailstorm of missiles. Elliot covered his ears, trying to block out the sound as they pummelled the giant relentlessly. Bang-bang-bang! Bang! Bang! How long before the machine man gave in?

To Elliot, trapped in the dark beneath the giant, with little space to move, each minute felt like an hour. But the machine man stood his ground. Elliot listened as the assault gradually grew weaker, quieter, less frequent over time. And finally, after what seemed like an eternity, it miraculously stopped altogether.

The butterflies had worn themselves out. They lingered for a while, then slowly moved off in search of easier prey.

Once the buzzing was completely gone, and the dust had fully settled, the machine man lifted his massive arm. Elliot could see Yilba and the octopus standing in the moonlight, looking on in amazement. "I'm okay," he said.

Yilba grinned ear to ear.

"Incredible," said the octopus.

~~~

They carried rocks and sticks from the forest, marking the graves as best they could. It took a long time, but they helped the machine man complete his final task.

And when they were done, the giant sat on the edge of the fountain, releasing a burst of steam from his valves. Elliot inspected his fuel gauge. It was noticeably lower than before. "What are you going to do?" he asked.

"I will sit and wait for my fuel to run dry," said the machine man.

That was not a good idea, Elliot thought. "Why don't you come with us?" he suggested.

The machine man paused. "I cannot leave my master."

"Your master is gone," Yilba said, stepping in. "The boy is your new master now."

The machine man looked over at the grave. Elliot could hear the whir of micro-processors spinning inside the giant's head. "I don't need to be your master. You can make decisions for yourself," Elliot said. "Who knows, maybe we'll find some fuel along the way."

The machine man remained unresponsive, so Elliot tried a different tack. "Okay. You're a task machine, right?"

"That is correct."

"Can you perform a task for us, then?"

"All tasks must comply with sections 9 through 12 of the Laws of the Blue Kingdom," said the machine man.

"I'm pretty sure this will comply," said Elliot.

The machine man paused. "You may proceed with your request."

"Okay." Elliot rubbed his hands together and cleared his throat. "Come with us. Help us find our way home."

The machine man sat for a while longer, microprocessors whirring on overdrive. Then, finally, the giant stood and looked down upon the boy, like a monolith blocking out the moon. "TM920, now accepting task #872," he said.

Elliot smiled.

FLOWERS

And so, three became four. Although the machine man was built like a tank, he was able to climb over logs and boulders, across streams and gullies, better than just about anyone. He had surprising agility, Elliot thought. Which made sense. He was a task machine, after all, and tasks came in many different shapes and sizes.

"TM920 isn't much of a name," said Elliot. "Why don't we call you Tim?"

Tim nodded.

On they went.

Elliot noticed their rations were getting thin. He made a joke about it: "Looks like our fuel's running low, too, Tim." But Tim didn't seem to find that funny. When Elliot asked him why, Tim admitted he didn't find anything funny. He wasn't programmed to.

Eventually, the trees grew thin, and the plants disappeared, and there wasn't much left but the ground beneath their feet. Off in the distance, an enormous structure came into view. It looked like a great wall, stretching as far as the eye could see in both directions.

"The edge of the forest," Yilba said.

As they approached, Elliot could see that it wasn't a wall, but a dense row of flowers about half a mile deep. They were enormous and prehistoric looking, with giant white petals and long red stamens reaching skyward.

"How do we get through?" asked the octopus.

"We don't," said Yilba, walking up to one of the flowers and grabbing hold of its stem. Everyone watched as she climbed like an inchworm to the top, pulling herself onto the petals and climbing higher still, right to the tippity-top of one of the stamens. There, she began bouncing up and down.

"What is that woman doing?" whispered the octopus.

"We don't go through, we go over!" she yelled, bouncing higher and higher, until, with one final push, she launched into the air. Elliot gasped, watching as Yilba bounced from flower to flower, vaulting into the distance.

"Shellen's beak, they're like trampolines!" blurted the octopus. The mollusc ran up to a flower, wrapped his tentacles around it, and scrambled up the stem. Once at the top of the stamen, he balanced himself, then started bobbing vigorously. "Ha-ha! Yes! Yes!" he cried. "They are! They're like trampolines!" Then he flew into the air. "*YEEEEEESSSS!*" he howled, leaping away with pure delight, twisting, twirling, and striking balletic poses as he went.

Elliot turned to Tim with excitement. "Do you think you can do that?" he said.

"I will try," Tim answered.

Each climbed their own flower, and when Elliot reached the top, he waited for Tim to catch up, surprised the flower could hold the machine man's considerable weight.

"I'll go first," Elliot said. He began to bounce. The stamen was elastic and rubbery, like a loaded spring. Once he'd gained enough momentum, he counted down: "Four ... Three ... Two ... One ... *Geronimooo!*" And off he shot with all his might.

For a moment, Elliot was floating weightless and free,

high above a sea of white petals. Then he felt that tickle in his belly, and he started falling back down, landing on a flower and bouncing until he settled safely. "Ha-ha! That was amazing! Go on, try it!" he called to Tim.

While Tim's face was incapable of expression, it was clear from his body language that he was feeling more than a little trepidation.

"It's okay, you can do it! Just bounce, and let the flower do the rest!"

Tim tested the waters, bending his knees a little.

"That's it!" Elliot encouraged.

As the machine man gained confidence, he started bouncing. A little at first, then a lot.

"Yeah! Keep going!" Elliot figured Tim needed all the praise he could get.

With each thrust, the giant climbed higher and higher, until it was time for him to launch.

"Go for it!" yelled Elliot.

And Tim went for it. He *really* went for it. He catapulted straight up like a rocket to the stratosphere, so high, Elliot wasn't sure if he'd ever come back down. But come back down he did, fast and furiously, crashing through the petals, straight to the ground.

"Tim!" screamed Elliot. He clambered down the stem and rushed over to find his friend upside down, with his head buried in the ground. Then, slowly but surely, Tim managed to pull himself out and stand. He staggered a bit.

"Tim, your head!" said Elliot, noticing it was on backward. Tim grabbed his head and spun it around, locking it into place.

"Are you okay?" asked Elliot.

Tim took a moment to recalibrate. "All systems are operational."

"Oh, thank goodness."

Elliot looked around. They were standing under a canopy of petals, surrounded by a forest of tall stems, making Elliot feel very much like a garden ant. He took Tim by the hand and led him through, calling out for their friends as they went. When he heard Yilba and the octopus answering back, he located the way out. They found the old woman and the octopus waiting for them, standing on the edge of a desert that stretched clear to the horizon.

They had reached the dunes.

THE DUNES

Elliot was stunned by the enormity of it all. Not just the sloping valleys and rolling hills, but the sky. There was so much of it. He could see the colossal dome shape it formed, and how it wrapped around the whole of the planet he stood upon. Looking up made him feel not just small, but invisible: a microscopic speck on a marble tumbling through space.

As they made their way across the barren landscape, beneath the illunas and the stars, Elliot began to notice objects buried in the sand: a stop sign, a dog bowl, an eagle's nest, a melting clock, a mannequin with eyes that seemed to follow him as they walked. The desert was littered with dream objects, partially covered over by wind and time.

The most impressive of all was something he came

across while climbing over the crest of a sandhill: a massive oil tanker sitting half-sunken in the sand. It was bigger than any ship Elliot had ever seen—the size of several football stadiums. But size wasn't even its most remarkable attribute. It had been painted hot pink, with rainbows, unicorns, and glittering hearts.

Who had dreamt of such a thing, and why? What had been going on inside that illuna before it broke apart? Elliot had no time to ponder. A sound rang out, one he'd heard only once before, but would be hard-pressed to ever forget.

Bwong!

He looked up. A pocket of spheres was churning in the sky, like waves on a stormy sea. *Bwong-bwong! Bwooong!* They were colliding with one another.

"Swim for shelter!" screamed the octopus, running away.

"Is it happening?" Elliot asked. "Are they going to fall?"

"Looks that way," said Yilba.

"What should we do?"

She smiled calmly. "Relax and enjoy the show."

Elliot looked back up, as a wave of epic proportions

crashed in on itself and shook loose the stars. Or at least, that's what it looked like, as thousands of glowing orbs exploded in the sky. They fell slowly downward, floating like fireworks through the night, their warm light illuminating the desert, and casting dancing shadows across the dunes. They fell all around them, and when they touched the ground, they disappeared, depositing their objects in the sand: a bell, a pillow, an apple, a rock, a tree, a bush, and something else, something alive—a deer: a huge grey buck standing atop a dune in utter confusion.

"Where am I?" said the deer, having awoken to find itself in another world.

"It's all right," said Elliot. "There's nothing to be afraid of."

The deer was very obviously in shock. "How is it I can understand you?" it said, astonished to be comprehending human speech.

"Everyone can understand everyone here," said Elliot, proud to finally know more about this world than someone else, for a change. "It's okay, you'll get used to it."

"Oh, no," said the deer, clearly not getting used to it at all. "*No-no-no-no-no.*"

"Try to stay calm. We can help," said Elliot. But the deer panicked and ran off, as fast as its legs would carry it. "Wait! Come back!" yelled Elliot, but that only made the deer run faster. "Stay away from butterflies!" Elliot shouted.

"Quiet!" Yilba scolded. "Voices carry in the desert."

As the animal disappeared into the distance, Elliot prayed it would avoid the butterflies, and whatever else might be lurking out there in the dark.

~~~

Elliot lay on his back next to Yilba, staring up at the illunas in the sky, those dream-spheres from another world—*his* world. How he wished he could jump up and grab hold of one, and travel back with it through time and space, back to where he belonged. His heart ached for home.

"Why are you doing this?" he asked.

"Doing what?" said Granny Yilba.

"Taking us to the mountain."

"Why wouldn't I?"

"Well, you hardly know us. You're risking your life for a couple of strangers."

Yilba paused. "Let's just say I want to help."

"Because of the vision I had? The ship on fire?"

She sighed and shook her head, smiling affectionately. "You really are a persistent one, aren't you?" Then she turned her gaze back toward the night sky.

Elliot changed the subject. "Were you born in this world?" he asked.

"Yes. My mother and father weren't, though. They came from your world."

"They did?"

"Mm-hmm. They met here, fell in love, and decided never to go back."

"Why?"

"Because everything they wanted was here. Each other."

That made little sense to Elliot. He couldn't fathom never wanting to go back, never missing home. He missed everything about home. He missed his family, his friends, his dog, his school, his neighbourhood, his room, his glow-in-the-dark stars. He even missed the way his house smelled (a bit like his mother's perfume). He missed how his family would sit around the fireplace in the wintertime, roasting marshmallows indoors. How his mother would bring him soup when he stayed home from school, and how soothing it was. He'd have done anything for a bowl of that soup right now. Anything in the whole world. He pictured his mother carrying a bowl toward him through the moonlight, and then hugging her and never letting her go.

His chest tightened and his eyes welled with tears. "I want my mom," he said. Then he started to cry.

"Oh, sweetheart, there, there," Yilba said, wrapping her arms around him and holding him tight. "I envy you, Elliot."

"You do?"

"I do. You have your whole life ahead of you. I'm at the opposite end, you see, looking back. And if I squint hard enough, I can see you standing there at the crossroads."

"The crossroads?" Elliot said with a sniffle.

"The paths we choose in life. They're all around us, everywhere. Some you can see, others you can't. And those are the tricky ones, the ones hiding in plain view."

"What do you mean?"

She let him go, adjusting her position in the sand and getting comfortable. "Let's say you were walking home and happened upon an ice-cream store. Do you go in?"

"Yes."

"Of course you do. You go in and walk straight up to the girl behind the counter, and ask for a scoop of strawberry ice cream."

"Just one?" said Elliot.

"Good point. Four."

"*Four* scoops?"

"Life is short. The girl gives y—"

"Wait," said Elliot, stopping her. "Could it be salted caramel? Salted caramel's my favourite."

"Sure. You order five scoops of salted caramel."

"You said four."

"Five's better. She gives you the ice cream, you give her your money, and off you go on your merry way. The entire exchange takes no more than two and a half minutes. When you get home, you say hello to your mother, she gives you a kiss, you do your homework, eat your dinner, and the rest of your life plays out pretty much the way you always expected it to, pleasantly and without a whole lot of surprises." Yilba nodded—*end of story.*

"That's it?" said Elliot.

"That's it."

"I don't understand."

"Well ..." She shifted her position in the sand again. "Let's say you ordered strawberry, instead."

"Okay."

"The girl behind the counter says they're out of strawberry, but not to worry, they have another tub in the back. So, off she goes to the freezer, gets out the stepladder, climbs to the top shelf, and takes down a new vat. She carries it out, plunks it into the cooler, removes the lid, and serves you six scoops of strawberry."

"Six, now?"

"By the time you get your cone, it's been seven minutes since you ordered, which means it's now twelve o'clock, the time her boss arrives. In he walks, sees you standing there with your eight scoops, and thinks, that kid sure loves strawberry. He lets you know strawberry is his favourite flavour. He adores it. Borders on an obsession. You tell him you think his strawberry ice cream is the best you've ever tasted—best in the world—which in turn, leads to him letting you in on a little secret. He's always dreamt of opening an All-Strawberry Store."

"What's that?"

"Exactly what it sounds like—a store that sells all things strawberry. Strawberry tarts, strawberry shortcakes, strawberry lollipops, strawberry jam, gum, salad, toast—"

"Toast?"

"—tea, wine, hats—you name it, they sell it. And if they don't, they make it for you on the spot. Well, golly, that's the best idea you've ever heard, you say, and you can't imagine anyone thinking otherwise. Unless they'd never tasted strawberry, or they were a strawberry, which makes him laugh. He takes a shine to you and offers you a summer job. You accept, and work there for several years. You never miss a day, and you work hard, eventually getting promoted to manager. You become close with your boss over time. He says you're the nearest thing he's ever had to a son. His daughter, who happens to be the smartest, funniest, loveliest person you've ever met, visits occasionally, and, needless to say, you fall in love. The two of you get married, and that turns your boss into your father-in-law. Years go by, as they do, and the time comes for your father-in-law to retire. Naturally, he hands the business over to his daughter and to you, which makes you ..."

"The boss?"

"The boss! Indeed. And as the boss, your first decision is to make your father-in-law's dream come true."

"The All-Strawberry Store?"

"The same. You invest money, time, blood, sweat, tears, and, after too much coffee and too little sleep, you find yourself standing in front of a crowd on opening day. It's time to cut the ribbon. Which you do. The doors open, and ..." She stopped.

"What? What happens?" said Elliot.

"The store is a huge success."

"Oh, phew."

"People come from all around to taste that pink gold. They call you the *Strawbarron*. You become fabulously wealthy, travel the world, have seven children, and retire on a private island in the middle of the ocean, all because you chose strawberry instead of salted caramel."

Elliot was stunned. "Oh, wow. I ..." He hadn't seen that coming.

"These paths are everywhere, Elliot, all around us. Most you can't see, but some you can, and it's those you must choose wisely, because even the slightest variation between one path and another, at your end, becomes a chasm by the time it gets to mine. The choices you make echo through time, louder with each passing year."

"But, how do you know what path to choose, if you don't even know where it leads?"

"Know what lights your heart. Allow that to guide you. Just don't mistake your heart for someone else's. And never let anyone choose for you. Only you can know your true path."

Elliot understood. He tucked his hands behind his head and looked back up at the sky. "Well, I'm definitely not having seven children."

Granny Yilba smiled. "There you go, see? You're already on your way."

THE RANCHER

Suddenly, a large animal appeared over the top of a dune, rearing up on its hindlegs. Tim bolted to his feet and stood in front of the group, shielding them. At first, they thought it was a lion, but then realized it wasn't even a cat. It was a kitten, a humungous fluffy kitten, eyes reflecting the light of the moon. A man was riding on its back, pointing a rifle.

"Git out from behind the robot with yer hands up, bootlickers!" the man hollered. "Come on, git!"

The group remained huddled together behind Tim.

"He's going to shoot," whispered Elliot.

"He can't shoot through solid metal," Granny Yilba whispered. Then she called out, "Put the gun down!"

"I weren't born yesterday," the man called back, spitting off to the side. "Ima count to three'n if ya don't come out, you'll be tasting hot lead! One!"

"Cover your ears," Yilba said to Elliot.

"Two!"

Elliot covered his ears.

"Three!"

They waited. Then they waited some more. But no shots were fired. The man called out again: "How come ya ain't a-shootin'?"

"Because we don't have any guns!" Yilba called back.

"We're just a boy, an old lady, and an octopus!" Elliot yelled.

"Ain't ya with the Bonney Boys?"

"No!" Yilba yelled.

"Who ya with, then?"

"No one!"

Silence. Then, "All right. Ima put my gun down. No shootin'. Promise."

Yilba motioned for Elliot and the octopus to stay put, then she stepped out from behind Tim.

"*Yilba,*" whispered Elliot, concerned for her safety. But she stood out in the open, assessing the situation, and after a moment, waved for them to join her. Cautiously, Elliot stepped out, then the octopus, and

they stood looking at the man who rode the giant kitten. He was rugged and dusty, wearing chaps and a big sombrero.

"What the heck is that?" said the man, pointing at the octopus.

"I'm an octopus," said the octopus.

"Well, I'll be. An octopus wearin' cowboy boots." The man slipped out of his saddle. "Look'ee here, folks— ma'am—my sincerest apologies. I thought y'all were poachers. May I approach?"

"As long as it's without that gun," said Yilba.

"Of that I can assure, ma'am. I ran outta' bullets years ago. Couldn't shoot if I tried."

"Me run now!" blurted the giant kitten, in an impossibly high voice, its eyes tweaking with pent-up energy. "Me run NOW!" it yelled again, nosing toward the open sands.

"No, Sundancer! Stay!" said the man, pulling the kitten's reins and bringing its head closer to his own. He whispered in its ear, and almost immediately, as though a switch had been flicked, the animal relaxed. The kitten curled up in the sand and started purring.

The man removed his hat and approached the group,

introducing himself with jangling spurs and an out-stretched hand. "Sing-Song Pete," he said.

"Granny Yilba. This is Elliot, Tim, and ... Octopus."

"Howdy," said Pete, shaking their hands, although when he got to the octopus, he didn't quite know what to do, so he just petted him on the head, instead. "If ya don't mind me askin,' what're y'all doin' out in the middle of the desert?"

"We're on our way to a mountain," said Yilba.

"Ya don't say. Well look, I feel somethin' awful, pullin' a gun on ya like that. Lemme make it up to ya, by inviting ya'll to my ranch for supper." He put his hand over his heart. "I can guarantee a good night's sleep and a full belly. What do ya say?"

Yilba glanced at Elliot, who wasn't about to pass up a hot meal and a warm bed. He nodded. "Okay, sounds good," Yilba said.

"Hot dog! Let's go!" Pete turned and strutted up the bank to his waiting kitten. The others followed. When they got to the top, they saw there were two more kittens, down on the other side, milling about, one white, one black.

"That down there's Whipped Cream and Night Dust.

This is Sundancer. Ever ride kittenback?"

"Can't say we have," said Yilba.

"They ride free and fierce, but don't worry, if ya fall, the sand'll catch ya."

Pete lifted the octopus onto Sundancer's back. Elliot and Yilba mounted Whipped Cream, and Tim climbed onto Night Dust, the largest of the three.

The kittens crouched down, bellies pressed against the sand, muscles tensed, pupils dilated. They appeared ready to explode. "Run!" "Attack!" "Pounce!" they mewed with their helium-high voices.

"Don't mind them," Pete said. "They're just babies is all, single-minded, and not the deepest of thinkers. They live in the moment. Okay, remember to hold tight. Ya don't wanna be gettin' whiplash."

"Shellen help us," prayed the octopus.

"Yaw!" hollered Pete, digging in his heels. Sundancer leapt forward, and in a burst of sand, Whipped Cream and Night Dust erupted behind her. They tore off across the plains, and whether it was from the excitement of it all, or just the stark-white fear, all five riders screamed in unison. Even Pete.

THE RANCH

The kittens were like three lunatic bullets searing across the moonlit landscape.

"Tell them to slow down!" yelled Granny Yilba.

"This *is* them slow!" Pete yelled back. Then he sang, with a voice so shrill it made the kittens shriek. "*What keeps the herd from runnin', stampedin' far and wide, the cowboy's long, low whistle, and singin' by their side!*"

"Quiet or you'll get us killed!" hollered Yilba.

"Don't worry! Ain't no creature livin' can outrun my kittens!" Pete yelled back.

On they charged across the desert. Every now and then, they'd stop to pounce on things that weren't there, but the kittens were so fast, they were able to cross great distances in a short amount of time, and it wasn't long before they reached their destination.

The ranch was located in the middle of a dried-up lakebed, surrounded by miles of flat ground. A tall wooden fence ran the length of the property, penning in scores of giant kittens, every shape and shade imaginable. Some were wrestling with each other, while others were drinking milk from steel basins, or napping on blankets.

On the roof of a farmhouse sat a girl scanning the horizon with a pair of binoculars. She waved as they approached. Another girl, busy corralling kittens on the ground below, came running to greet them.

"Daddy! Who'd you bring?"

"Woah!" Pete hollered, pulling back on the reins. "Just some folks I met out in the desert. Thought we'd show 'em what authentic frontier hospitality looks like." He turned to the group. "Everyone, this is Amelia, the apple of my eye."

"Hello," said Amelia, who wore overalls and had freckles.

"Pleased to meet you," said Elliot.

Pete pointed up at the roof. "That there's the apple of my *other* eye, Penelope." Elliot glanced up, but before he could wave hello, a horrendous shriek rang out.

"Daddy! Jitterbug's freaking out again!" cried Amelia. And with that, Pete was off, leaping over fences and running across the ranch, toward a wild-eyed kitten standing tall on two legs, threatening another with its claws.

Amelia moved next to Elliot. "Watch this," she said, leaning in.

Pete jumped onto the kitten's back and whispered into its ear. He scratched behind its neck, and pressed his thumb into a spot between its eyes, and within seconds, Jitterbug relaxed, settling down and curling up into a purring ball of fur.

"My dad's a kitten whisperer," Amelia said proudly. "Best there ever was. Probably the last now, too."

Pete motioned for them to follow. "Come on inside. I'll introduce you to my wife."

They entered the house. It was warm and inviting, lit by oil lamps, and smelling of baked bread. In the kitchen was a woman, busy cleaning out the chimney of a wood-burning stove.

"Ginny, look what I found," Pete announced. "Company!"

The woman stopped what she was doing and turned.

"Oh, for goodness' sake," she said, with a look of surprise.

"Folks, this is Virginia, the light of my life."

Virginia wiped the ash from her hands and fixed her hair. "I can't tell you how long it's been since we've had guests," she said. "And look at me, all covered in soot."

"Never mind that, dear, you look lovely," said Yilba.

"We appreciate your having us," said the octopus.

"It's our pleasure," said Virginia. "What brings you to the middle of nowhere?"

"We're on our way to a mountain," said Elliot. "We were camping out in the desert when, all of a sudden, Pete showed up, pointing a gun, and we just about had a heart attack." He chuckled, finding it funny now.

But Virginia didn't appear to find it funny at all. "He did *what?*"

"Honey, I thought they was the Bonney Boys," said Pete.

"*The Bonney Boys?* We haven't seen them in years, Peter. They're gone, just like everybody else. What's the matter with you?"

"I know, I know. I'm sorry." He turned to the group. "Y'all have no idea what trouble them boys used to cause us. It ain't no—"

"And stop with the *y'all* this and *ain't* that!" Virginia said. "You're a kitten rancher, not a cowboy, for goodness' sake. And take off that ridiculous hat."

Pete removed his sombrero.

Virginia shook her head. "I apologize for my husband. He marches to the beat of a different drummer. Now, let's get you a drink. You must be parched."

~~~

Dinner was served on a harvest table: preserved peaches, preserved lemons, pickled carrots, pickled onions, pickled cabbage, pickled pickles, and the pièce de résistance: a can of baked beans they'd saved for a special occasion.

"Apologies for the slim pickings," said Pete. "As you know, food's not exactly plentiful these days. We're just lucky Ginny was an avid canner. Enough in the basement to last us ..." he glanced over at his daughter, who looked concerned, "... a long time."

"It's wonderful," said Yilba. "Thank you all for your generosity."

Elliot noticed that only Amelia was seated at the

table. "Will Penelope be joining us?" he asked.

"Oh, you bet. In fact, she's already here," said Pete, pointing at Amelia—who was actually Penelope. *Identical twins.*

Penelope laughed at Elliot's confusion.

"Heck, I can't tell 'em apart, either," Pete said. "That's why Penelope wears a pink shirt and Amelia wears green."

Penelope smirked. "Or ... *do* we?"

"Now, don't be messin' with your daddy, sugar pie."

"Amelia's on the roof," Penelope explained. "We take turns."

"There's always someone up there watching," Pete added. "That's how we've been able to stay put, while everyone else had to go into hiding. You can see the little devils coming from miles away. Gives us enough time to round up the kittens and batten down the hatches." Pete walked over to a cabinet and brought out a bottle. "Now, this here I distill myself, right here on the ranch. True old-fashioned hooch." He poured a glass for Yilba, Virginia, and himself.

Virginia looked over at Tim, who was standing in a dark corner. "Would your friend like to join us?"

"He's trying to preserve fuel," said Elliot. "Actually, we were hoping we might find some. Do you have any ... I think it's called, bitonium?"

"No, I'm sorry. I wish I could say we did," said Pete.

The clanging of a bell sounded from the rooftop, causing Pete and his daughter to jump out of their chairs. "Whoop, here we go. Battle stations, everyone."

Elliot's heart quickened, watching as they grabbed lassos off a hook and rushed to the door.

"Is there anything we can do?" Yilba asked.

"Heck, yeah," said Pete. "Just stay here and enjoy the whiskey 'til we get back. We got this." And with that, Pete and Penelope slipped out the door.

Elliot felt sick with fear. He looked anxiously at Yilba.

"It's okay, you're safe in here, honey," said Virginia, sensing his unease. She moved from room to room, pulling metal reinforcements down over the windows and locking them into place, while outside, Pete and his daughters rounded up the kittens and corralled them into an underground bunker. It was a well-oiled operation they'd obviously performed hundreds of times. But it did little to quell Elliot's fear.

Yilba rubbed his shoulder. "It's all right," she re-assured him.

A few minutes later, Pete walked back in with Amelia and Penelope, and they sat at the table as the sound of buzzing rose up in the distance. It was ominous, like the approach of bomber jets.

"*Aaaand* … cue the critters," said Pete with a wink.

They crashed upon the house, pummelling the walls in a hailstorm of ferocity. Elliot gritted his teeth and covered his ears, feeling transported back to that dark and frightening place, trapped beneath the machine man. *Bang-bang! Bang-bang-bang! Bang!*

"You'd think by now, they'd have figured out they can't slam their beady little heads through a brick wall," said Pete. "Dumb as rocks, they are."

Elliot kept his ears covered, dampening the sound as best he could, and keeping his eyes on the floor.

"Is he all right?" Pete asked Yilba.

"He'll be fine. He's just not used to this. He's not from here."

"*Oooh.* I see," said Pete knowingly. He took a sip of his whiskey. "You know something, Elliot? I can't tell who's from here and who's not anymore. And if you ask me, there ain't much of a difference. In fact, some people think the ancients of this world came from yours, thousands of years ago."

Elliot looked up, while keeping his hands over his ears.

"Then there're those who think our worlds are merely reflections of one another—different versions of the same thing. Pretty wild, huh?"

Elliot nodded.

"You wanna know something else?"

"*Dad,*" Penelope said, rolling her eyes.

But Pete went on. "Some folks think there's more than one universe. Heck, they think there's a whole whack of 'em. An infinite number, side-by-side, with infinite versions of our worlds in 'em, and infinite you's and me's, infinite everybody's—every kind imaginable. Tall-you, small-you, fat-you, thin-you, cowboy-you, pirate-you, purple-you, you with two heads, you with eight legs. Because every moment branches off in infinite directions, creating new universes in turn, and taking—"

"Dad, stop, you're freaking him out!" said Amelia.

"Yeah, ease up on the whiskey, Peter," said Virginia.

"No, it's okay," said Elliot, who'd removed his hands from his ears and was listening intently now. "It's interesting."

"There, see?" Pete said, motioning to Elliot. "It's interesting. No one's freaking out here. Hey!" Pete slammed his hand on the table. "You ever heard the legend of Handsome Ned and the Beauty Baily?"

"You mean, the man who imprisoned the boy who wakes the sun?" said Elliot.

"So, you *have* heard it."

"No, not really. Granny Yilba only told me a little."

"Okay, well then, allow me to expound."

"Oh, no, he's going to expound," said Penelope under her breath.

Pete began. "Ned was born to the richest woman in Lappanthia. She'd made her fortune selling black magic to the Lords of the Three Kingdoms. They'd pay anything for it."

"Criminals," muttered Yilba.

"She spoiled Ned rotten," Pete went on. "Bought him anything his heart desired, and I do mean anything."

"Like what?" asked Elliot.

"Like a pirate ship, for one, complete with working cannons. But what Ned loved more than anything, was beauty. He was obsessed with it. And the most beautiful thing in the world to him was the butterfly. His mother bought him every kind imaginable. Spared no expense. Only problem was, Ned hadn't the knowledge nor the ability to care for the critters, so they brought in a girl from the village to look after them."

Pete stood and moved around the table, making dramatic gestures with his arms. "Stars above. Ned thought he'd seen it all, until he saw her. She was so beautiful, she outshone the sun—which did shine brightly in those days. Her name was Baily, but to Ned, she was the only creature more beautiful than his beloved butterflies."

Yilba coughed.

"You okay?" asked Elliot. She nodded.

"He took her on his pirate ship," Pete continued, "and they sailed the world, falling in love through a series of adventures, getting married, and living happily— although unfortunately, not *ever after*. For Baily, you see, still had feelings for the boy she left behind. She longed for his embrace, and one night by the light of the moon, she left. Ned was devastated. So distraught was he, that he broke into his mother's lab, and wielded her darkest of magics, turning the butterflies into the soul-destroying demons we know today. He sent them off into the world to spread their mortal sorrow, so that every living thing might know his pain, the pain that Baily had brought him."

"Wow," said Elliot. "That's very dramatic."

"Ain't it? All true, too."

"No, it's not," Yilba interjected.

Pete paused. "What do you mean?"

She poured herself another whiskey. "That's not what happened."

"Oh, really?" said Pete, sitting down and leaning back in his chair, folding his arms. "Pray tell then, what happened?"

Yilba gulped her whiskey, then plunked the glass down loudly on the table. She seemed to have something bubbling up inside her, Elliot thought. "Ned was so in love with himself," she said, "that he grew jealous of Baily, the only person more beautiful than him. Ned's beauty was on the surface, you see, while Baily's sprang from a well deep inside. He created the butterflies to make her miserable, in the hopes her beauty might fade and lessen in the face of his own. *That* was the reason she fled."

"Hmpf," Pete said. "I had not heard that."

"Well, now you have," said Yilba, staring at her glass. "Now you have."

PASSINGS

Elliot had been so wrapped up in the story of Handsome Ned and the Beauty Baily, he hadn't noticed the butterfly attack had ended, until now. He breathed a sigh of relief.

"So, what mountain are you headed to?" Virginia asked.

"Mount Valkrius," Yilba answered.

"Mount Valkrius? That's a long way. Why are you headed there, if you don't mind my asking?"

"Oh," said Elliot, piping in. "There's a gateway to our world at the top of the mountain."

"Our only way home," added the octopus.

"I see," said Pete. "Well, that's a pickle."

Virginia leaned into her husband. "Why don't you let them ride the tabbies?"

"What? Sweetheart, you can't just *ride the tabbies*. Can't just jump on a kitten and go."

"They rode here, didn't they?"

"Sure, because I was riding with them. Besides, how would they get back?"

"Yilba could bring them back."

Pete sighed. "I can't believe you're saying this, honey."

As Pete and Virginia continued to argue, Elliot decided to check on Tim. He excused himself and walked over to where the giant was standing.

"Tim, how are you doing?" he asked.

But the machine man didn't answer. Elliot looked at his gauge. His fuel had finally run dry. Tim was gone. He'd passed away quietly, alone in the corner, while they were having supper.

"Oh, no. Tim." Elliot wrapped his arms (not even halfway) around the machine man's body, and cried in the shadows so no one would see. He took a moment to pull himself together and wipe his tears away, but when he returned to the table, Yilba gave him a sharp look.

"What's wrong, dear?" she said.

Elliot paused. "Tim's gone."

"Oh, sweetheart." Yilba opened her arms and pulled him close.

"He's gone?" said Pete, looking over at the corner. "Ah, dang it, Tim, we hardly knew ya." The rancher stood and raised his glass. "To Tim. May he rest in peace, in robot heaven."

"To Tim," they said, clinking their glasses.

Pete rubbed his forehead. "Now, how the heck am I gonna get him outta my living room?"

"Peter, that's not funny," said Virginia. "Show some respect, the boy's upset."

"Apologies," Pete said.

Amelia went over to the window. She unlocked the metal barricade and lifted it up. Leaning out into the dry, moonlit air, she took a deep breath.

Then suddenly, she screamed.

Everyone jumped out of their chairs and rushed over to join her, but Amelia was already gone, running out the door and across the yard to a kitten, who lay motionless in the sand.

"Jitterbug!" Penelope screamed. She ran after her sister, and they all went out and gathered around the kitten. The girls threw themselves on the animal, their tears melting into its fur.

"How could this happen?" cried Amelia.

"He must have hidden in the silo again," said Virginia, hand clasped over her mouth.

"No! I checked! I counted, I swear!" cried the girl.

Pete knelt down and whispered into Jitterbug's ear.

"Come on, Daddy, you can do it!" said Penelope.

The girls held onto their mother, and they all watched as Pete whispered. He whispered and whispered. He whispered with all the spirit he could muster. But it wasn't enough. The kitten had stopped breathing. Pete shook his head.

"NO!" cried Amelia. The girls wept inconsolably.

"We should get back inside," said Yilba, reminding them that, at some point soon, the butterfly would exit the animal's body, and it wasn't safe to be around.

They returned to the house, taking extra care to barricade the doors and windows. There had been enough death for one night.

RESURRECTION

They held a funeral for Jitterbug the next day. Penelope and Amelia both gave eulogies, recounting the kitten's wild, vibrant life. He would leave a desert-sized hole in their hearts, they said, and they would miss him dearly. After lowering his coffin into the ground, they placed a grave-marker in the sand. It read:

Here lies Jitterbug,
whose paw prints will forever be
emblazoned upon our hearts.
Rest in peace.

After the funeral, they went inside. Virginia sat next to the fire, Pete and the girls at the kitchen table, and Elliot, Yilba, and the octopus grouped together in the living room. No one spoke. The only sound was from a marble being rolled back and forth across the table between Penelope's fingers. *Back ... and forth. Back ... and forth. Back ... and forth.* It was lulling, and hypnotic ... until it stopped.

Elliot glanced over at Penelope. She was looking at her father, who was sitting upright in his chair, eyes darting back and forth, lost deep in thought.

"What is it, Daddy?" she said.

Pete pushed his chair back, stood up, and walked briskly to a bookshelf. There, he took out an encyclopedia and started flipping through the pages, muttering to himself. "Basket weaving ... Beachcombers ... Bentgrass ... Biteplates ... Aha!" he blurted out. "Bitonium!"

Elliot snapped to attention.

"Uh-huh. Yep. Here we are," said Pete, moving his finger across the lines of text.

Elliot went and looked over his shoulder. "What does it say?"

"Just what I thought," Pete said, tapping his finger on the page. "Bitonium's ammonia-based."

"What does that mean?"

Pete looked at him with a spark in his eye. "You know what else is ammonia-based?"

"No."

"Cat pee."

Elliot smiled.

~~~

They worked into the night, gathering the kittens' urine, and pouring it into Pete's distiller, heating it to a boil, and sending it through a condenser to a receiving flask, where it cooled. Once it was ready, they poured the liquid into Tim's intake valve.

"How long before we know if it works?" said Elliot.

"Beats me." Pete shrugged. "I reckon this is the first time anyone's tried powering a robot with cat pee. Your guess is as good as mine."

They waited. And as they waited, Pete sang. Terribly.

"*Some cowboys ride for pleasure, they've got this whole thing wrong, I ride my gosh darn kittens, and sing to them this song! Yippee-ti-yo! Git along little kitties!*"

"Dad, stop!" begged Penelope.

Elliot kept his eyes on Tim, watching for signs of life, any lurch or twitch, anything to show that it might be working. But the machine man remained perfectly still. And as the minutes ticked by, Elliot began to lose hope. *What are we doing?* he wondered. *Are we out of our minds?* His heart sank. It was clear this wasn't going to work. He turned around and shuffled out of the room. But as he rounded the corner, Amelia shouted, "Look!"

Elliot rushed back in. Amelia was pointing at Tim's gears. They were moving! The machine man's motors were humming back to life. His head started rotating back and forth in fits and spurts.

Tim was back.

"TM920, now operational and ready for service," he announced.

"Tim, it's me!" shouted Elliot, jumping for joy.

"Elliot?" said the giant. "Did you find bitonium?"

"Well, um ..." said the boy, guiltily. "Sort of."

~~~

They celebrated with a late-night shindig. Pete brought out his special-reserve whiskey and cowboy records, and everyone danced into the night. Pete and the girls did the two-step; Yilba taught Elliot the cancan; and the octopus danced the funky shuffle. Virginia spun Tim around on the dance floor and, in that moment, decided he should live with them on the ranch. It only made sense, she claimed. So long as there were kittens, there'd be fuel for him to live on, and seeing as though the chores on a ranch never ended, having a Haminian Task Machine around would be a godsend.

After an hour or so, Yilba retired to the couch, the octopus to the bathtub, and Elliot to a mattress on the living room floor. Tim, who didn't require sleep, stayed up all night, shovelling cat poop, out by the barn.

Elliot lay, listening to the sounds of the shovel scraping against the sand as he drifted off. It was soft and rhythmic. Relaxing. And before he knew it, all thoughts of the journey ahead melted away.

Elliot dreamt of home that night.

When he awoke, it was to the smell of coffee, and for a moment, he thought he was back in his room, with his mother downstairs making breakfast. He lay with his eyes closed for a while, breathing it all in, not wanting to spoil the moment. And when he finally opened them, he saw he was not in his room, but rather, in a farmhouse on a giant kitten ranch in another world, and it was time to get up.

Elliot went into the kitchen, where he found Virginia preparing a plate of leftovers for him: pickled eggs, pickled onions, and the last of the beans. He thanked her, dug in, and swiftly cleaned his plate.

"Where'd everybody go?" he asked.

"They're outside getting ready."

"For what?"

She smiled. "Come and see."

He followed her outside. Yilba, Tim, the octopus, and the girls were watching Pete tack up Sundancer and three sleek-looking tabbies.

Pete looked over. "I'll take you as far as the mountain," he said. "After that, you're on your own."

Elliot smiled at his good fortune. "Thank you," he said.

"Nah, we should be thanking you," said Pete. "You've given us an enormous gift in the form of Tim.

Taking you to the mountain is the least we could do." He pointed at the tabbies. "These are my fastest rides. Firefly, Mystery Train, and Tiger Lily. They're all kinds of whacko, but they'll never let you down."

He fastened their saddles, then it was time to say goodbye. Elliot hugged Virginia and the girls, and moved on to Tim.

"Elliot, has task #872 been completed to your satisfaction?" Tim asked.

"Yes, Tim. Very much," said Elliot.

Tim paused. "Very well. Task #872 now being logged as complete."

Elliot smiled, holding back tears. "You'll be happy here. I know you will." He hugged Tim one last time, then saddled up and rode off.

As Elliot and his kitten passed through the gateway of the ranch, Elliot looked back one last time, and saw Tim standing there, holding a shovelful of poop, and while it didn't seem plausible or at all correct, Elliot could swear the machine man was smiling.

THE VALLEY

The kittens rode roughshod across the dunes on the greatest mission of all time (which was every mission, according to them). Pete sang and it wasn't pretty, and every now and then they'd stop to rehydrate, get back in their saddles, and ride on.

After a while, Elliot saw Mount Valkrius come into view, with its towering peaks rising above the clouds. It was bigger and even more impressive than he'd seen in his vision. Excitement grew inside him. *They were almost there.* All they had to do was make it through the valley. But, unlike the wide-open desert, the valley was rife with places for enemies to hide. Bushes and thickets created shadowy nooks everywhere you looked.

The kittens crept slowly along the riverbank, staring up at the trees, which stood like giant sentries in the moonlight, watching them pass.

"My tentacles are tingling," said the octopus. "I don't like this place."

"I don't like it, either," said Elliot.

Yilba remained on high alert, turning her head this way and that, listening with her hearmuffs.

"Elliot?" whispered the octopus.

"Yeah?"

"If anything happens ... I want you to know, I consider you a great friend. I'm lucky to have met you."

"I'm lucky to have met you, too," Elliot whispered back. "But this is not goodbye. We're going to make it."

"Quiet back there," Pete whispered from the front.

They continued along in silence, until Sundancer piped up. "Don't like," she said with her high voice.

"Don't like what?" said Pete.

"Bad," said the kitten, as she stopped and arched her back, fur standing on end. "Go back."

"What is it, Sunny? What's got you spooked?"

"Tree," said the kitten.

"What tree?" said Pete, frantically looking around.

"Bad tree," said Sundancer. She began to hiss, and

the other kittens started hissing along with her.

"I think it's time to go," said the octopus, burrowing into his kitten's fur.

Elliot looked around, and noticed a tree that was different from all the others. The top didn't come together into a point, but rather, spread outward into a heart shape.

"That one," said Elliot, pointing up at it.

"Ain't no treetop," said Pete.

The dark shape began to move, expanding outward, unfolding into a new shape—the shape of wings. Butterfly wings.

Elliot gasped. "BUTTERFLY!" he screamed.

Pete turned the kittens around, hollering, "Yaw! Yaw!" as the demon launched from the treetop, its bloodred eyes locking onto Elliot as it swooped downward.

The terrified kittens ran along the riverbank, ears folded back against their heads, bodies stretched long and lean, like four furry missiles speeding through the night. Pete drove them forward, while everyone else held on for dear life.

The kittens swiftly left the creature in the dust. They turned off the path and ran into the bushes, scrambling

through a maze of underbrush, darting this way and that, staying close together and low to the ground. Leaves smacked Elliot's face as they flew by. The kittens circled back and re-emerged along the riverbank, running at breakneck speed.

Elliot, who was last in line, glanced back over his shoulder, and saw the butterfly chasing after them. It was even further behind now, and soon it would be lost altogether. He breathed a sigh of relief—*they were going to be okay*—but then he looked up ahead. There was a fallen tree blocking their path.

"Hang on everybody!" Pete screamed.

They were going to jump it.

Elliot said a prayer as his kitten barrelled headlong toward the obstacle. Sundancer and Pete jumped first, clearing it with ease. Then Firefly and Yilba went, leaping over the tree as well. Next was Mystery Train and the (screaming) octopus, and they, too, made it over—but just barely.

And then, finally, it was Elliot and Tiger Lily's turn. Elliot could feel the kitten's nervousness as they approached. "You can do it! You can do it!" he told her.

Then he closed his eyes ... and they were airborne.

And Tiger Lily made it!

But when she landed, she twisted her paw, crying out in pain.

"No!" shouted Elliot. The kitten was now limping, struggling to keep pace. "Faster! Faster!" he yelled, jabbing his heels into her ribs. But they steadily fell behind. The butterfly was gaining.

The octopus—riding the kitten up ahead—looked back at Elliot. "Jump Elliot! Jump off!" he screamed.

But Tiger Lily stumbled, and Elliot was hit.

THE OCEAN

Elliot lay slumped across Sundancer's back, tied to the saddle. And while his eyes were open and his heart was beating, he was really only half-alive, buried beneath a merciless dark. The octopus rode with him, muttering words into his ear.

"Focus on what makes you happy, Elliot."

But Elliot could not. He could only feel a pain so great, it wasn't pain anymore, just an endless void torching his soul.

"Remember, I came through this, so can you. Listen to me," said the octopus.

He listened, and he heard the octopus's words, but retained none of their meaning. Nothing meant anything anymore. Nothing mattered. Nothing except release. Release from the pain.

"You're not going to slip away on me, you understand? I won't let you," the octopus told him.

Pete and Yilba followed close behind, looking on with concern. "Do you think he's going to make it?" asked Pete.

Yilba put her hand over her mouth. "I fear we're losing him," she said.

The octopus continued to talk. He talked about the ocean and the shore, about friends and trampolines, memorable meals and good naps, warm currents, selfless acts, and simple pleasures. He talked about swimming, and pancakes, and everything in between. He talked about anything and everything. But with each passing moment, his voice seemed farther and farther away. Occasionally, a word would get through: flying, dancing, sea foam. Rocks, was it? Elliot wished he was a rock—inanimate, unfeeling, and not alive.

Eventually, he couldn't hear the octopus at all. He couldn't see him, either. The octopus became a dot inside a pinhole, shrinking further into the distance. Darkness closed in all around Elliot, until there was nothing left but the hopeless eternity of sorrow by his side. He lay alone in a cold, black place.

Where was he?

What did it matter? He would lie and wait for the end to come. He only prayed it would arrive swiftly. Time slipped off in all directions, until a hole opened in his chest and out poured his soul, spilling onto the floor in a puddle in which he lay, numb and still.

Mom.

Dad.

Time to go.

A tear trickled from his eye, dissolving into an ocean of nothing.

An ocean.

Ocean.

What was that?

Ocean.

Was that him?

Ocean.

It was there in the faintest echo, like a flicker in the dark.

The ocean.

What of it?

It was vast and blue. Smelled of brine, sounded of

waves, tasted of salt. The ocean, with its push of current through his hair, across his face. Its coolness on his skin. The ocean and how it sparkled with life. It called to him, inviting him in. But Elliot was unable to move beneath the weight of his own pain. So, the ocean moved to him. It surrounded him and lifted him up, where he floated, weightless and free. He could see sand below him, and rocks, and coral, and fish. There were fish everywhere, swimming all around him, a myriad of colours, their eyes connecting with his own. Dolphins appeared, offering him their fins.

They swam together, Elliot and the dolphins, the powerful bodies of the marine mammals cutting through the water like torpedoes. Above, a slow-moving behemoth blocked out the sun. It was a whale shark. Elliot swam up and ran his fingers along the underside of its belly. How could such a thing exist? How could any of it exist? It was a miracle, the ocean. It filled him with joy. And its beauty crashed in against the dark.

A struggle took place between two forces, clashing furiously inside him.

Until one prevailed.

Elliot could hear his friends cheering from somewhere off in the distance. They were cheering for him. He would see them again.

He swam up, up, up, until he broke through the surface, and a blinding light met his eyes. Then suddenly, he was in the arms of his friends. Yilba was crying tears of joy, while Pete was wrestling on the ground with a thrashing backpack, containing the captured butterfly that had just escaped from Elliot's body.

"Welcome back," said the octopus.

THE MOUNTAIN

Elliot had regained much of his strength by the time they reached the mountain. He felt lucky to be alive, grateful to have made it through that dark and most terrible of places. He was recharged now, ready to take on anything. Even a mountain.

"Well, partners, it's been a heck of a ride," Pete said, halting the kittens.

"I don't know how to thank you," said Elliot.

"You don't have to. I just follow the kitten rancher code—*always harness the power of kittens for the betterment of all*—which is exactly what I did." He pulled back on Sundancer's reins, turning her around and, looking into the distance with a smile, he said, "I'm gonna write a song about us. I'll sing it across the land. We'll be legends."

Elliot watched the rancher ride off into the valley

with Firefly, Mystery Train, and Tiger Lily in tow, singing at the top of his lungs.

Badly.

~~~

They followed an alpine trail up through the evergreens and lichen-covered rocks. Elliot could see the diagonal opening in the mountain now, just as it had appeared in his vision. *They were so close.*

The angle steepened and the air grew thinner, and they made frequent stops to catch their breath or massage their aching legs. It was a tough climb, and Elliot thought it couldn't get much tougher, until they came to a massive body of rock that rose directly upward like a skyscraper, ending high up in the clouds. It was the upper region of the mountain. And it was also where the bodies lay.

Skeletons were strewn across the rocks, dressed in weathered clothing from different eras. Some looked like they'd been there for a year, others maybe a hundred or more—climbers who'd attempted to reach the summit, but had lost their footing and fallen from great heights.

Wreckages of flying machines lay all around as well—wild, propellered contraptions covered in rust and moss.

"M-maybe we should rethink this mountain-climbing thing," said the octopus.

"Take out your equipment," Yilba said, ignoring him. She demonstrated how to fasten a rope, and how to anchor a bolt into a rocky crevice. Elliot and the octopus practised until they got the hang of it. Then they gathered their climbing equipment (and their courage) and continued on.

The trail led to a wrought-iron archway, marking the start of a new path, one that wrapped around the massive rock like a spiral staircase. It was uneven and barely a foot in diameter, but it went up, and that was the way they needed to go.

Keeping their backs pressed against the rock, they shuffled along, sliding their feet sideways, which was especially heart-stopping in the low light, as it was hard to see the narrow ledge. But before they knew it, they were high above the ground.

"Don't look down," said Yilba.

Elliot stole a quick glance, but he wouldn't do it again. They were so high he nearly fainted. Far below, the skeletons lay in the moonlight, staring back up with their hollow sockets. "I will not become one of you," he whispered to himself.

When they entered the upper atmosphere, the world got cold. A light dusting of snow covered the rocks, and breathing became difficult, making the climb all the more treacherous. Just one slip would send any one of them plummeting. Elliot's teeth chattered and his hands shook, as much from the fear as the cold.

Then they entered the clouds, and were enveloped in a wash of mist that made it impossible to see anything beyond a few feet. Which was actually a blessing, Elliot thought, as now they couldn't see how high they were.

But as Elliot stared into the fog, he got the feeling they were being watched, as though there was something out there, lurking. It sent a chill down his spine.

Then he saw the mist start to move in strange and unnatural ways.

"The mist is moving! Look!" he said.

"Keep your eyes on the path, Elliot," Yilba responded.

"It's probably just your mind playing tricks on you," said the octopus. "Happens all the time when we swim between pressure zones. Things can get pretty entertaining."

Elliot looked again. The mist was clearly swirling and shifting, taking different forms as though it were alive. "It is. It's moving," he said.

Yilba stopped and she, too, stared into the mist. "Quickly. Anchor yourselves to the rock," she said.

"What is it?" said the octopus.

"Just do it!"

Elliot fumbled with his bolt and nearly dropped it, but he managed to secure himself to the mountain. Looking out, he saw several large forms taking shape.

"I can't attach my bolt!" screamed the octopus. Elliot shuffled over and helped his fingerless friend wedge the bolt into a crevice. "Look!" cried the octopus.

Ten figures made entirely of cloud vapour were hanging in the fog. They had pointed ears and ram-like horns.

"What are they?" said Elliot, his legs turning weak with fear.

"Cloud wraiths," Yilba said.

The ghostly creatures moved in circles, taking in huge gusts of air, and puffing out their chests like swollen balloons.

"They're gonna blow!" screamed the octopus.

"Hang on!" cried Yilba.

The wraiths exhaled, unleashing a violent windstorm, so powerful that chunks of loose rock came detached from the path around their feet, and blew away into the mist.

"We have to go back!" yelled the octopus.

"No!" said Yilba, her voice faint beneath the rushing of wind. "If we move, we fall! Hold tight!"

The wraiths blew harder, and the wind became a full-force gale. Elliot gripped the rock so tightly, his hands began to bleed. And as the creatures moved closer, the wind grew even stronger.

"I can't hold on!" yelled Elliot, his fingers growing weak. One of his hands came loose, then the other, then he screamed with terror as he fell from the ledge. But the rope snapped tight and held him. Yilba and the octopus fell next, and they all hung helplessly off the side of the mountain, blown around like bobbles on strings. The octopus slammed against the rock again and again, spraying black ink everywhere.

"I can't hold on!" yelled Elliot, his fingers growing weak.

How long before the bolts gave way? How long before they fell blindly into the mist?

Suddenly, the cloud creature with the tusk-like fangs called out, "*Stop!*"—its voice a mix of breath and echo. It floated toward Elliot, looking him up and down, while the others hung back, hovering in the air. "*Wake, Megusen,*" the creature announced.

"*Wake, Megusen. Wake, Megusen. Wake, Megusen,*" the others whispered. Then three broke away from the group and pushed off into the fog.

"Is everyone okay?" Yilba asked.

"Yes!" said Elliot.

"No!" said the octopus. "Feeling rather tenderized!"

"Why was it looking at me?" said Elliot, panic-stricken. "Who's Megusen?"

"I don't know. Just stay calm!" Yilba said.

A moment later, the wraiths returned, carrying an enormous trunk made of cloud. They set it down in the air and began to unlock it.

"What's in that?" cried Elliot.

"Stay calm, Elliot!" Yilba shouted.

The trunk began to open, letting loose an exhale of

gas, and a low rumble that shook Elliot to his core.

"What is it?!" Elliot choked.

"Stay calm!" said Yilba.

From out of the trunk rose a colossal cloud being. *"Megusen, Megusen, Megusen,"* the creatures chanted.

He was old and ancient, with a round belly, and a beard that billowed out in all directions. In the middle of his forehead was a third eye that remained shut. *"Why did you wake Megusen?"* came the mighty being's voice.

"The boy," said the wraith with the tusks.

Megusen stretched his neck and sat upright, tilting his head from side to side. Then the cloud king forced himself out of the trunk, spilling over the sides and floating up to Elliot, coming so close that each time he exhaled, it pushed Elliot back against the rock, then pulled him forward again, over and over like a pendulum.

Elliot felt like he was about to faint.

"Calm, Elliot!" yelled Yilba.

But calm was not possible. Not in the face of Megusen. The being's third eye began to open, and Elliot turned away, too frightened to look.

"Look into Megusen," said the giant. But Elliot dared not.

"Look into Megusen. Look into Megusen. Look into Megusen," the creatures whispered.

"No!" cried Elliot.

Megusen's breathing turned angry. *"LOOK INTO MEGUSEN!"* he roared, shaking the foundation of the mountain itself. Elliot screamed.

"For Shellen's sake, look into Megusen!" cried the octopus.

"Do it, Elliot!" shouted Yilba.

Elliot opened his eyes.

And suddenly, everything was quiet. Elliot was no longer tethered to the cliff. He was standing alone in a large empty room. *Was this another vision?* Out of the corner of his eye, he saw something move. A dark shadow swept across the wall. "Hello?" Elliot said, his voice echoing through the space.

A figure appeared from around the far corner. It was difficult to see at first, but as it moved toward him through the moonlight, Elliot could see it was a boy. He was about the same age as Elliot. He wore all black, and his eyes were shut. Was he sleepwalking? When the boy got to within a few feet, he stopped, and Elliot could see him clearly.

The boy looked exactly like Elliot.

He had a different haircut and wore different clothes, but other than that, he was exactly the same. It was eerie. The boy stood stock-still, eyes closed, facing Elliot.

"Who are you?" said Elliot.

The boy didn't answer.

"Are you ... me?" Elliot said.

With his eyes still closed, the boy pointed to the floor. Elliot looked down. There was an engraving embedded in the marble tile: a sun and moon, side-by-side. Elliot looked back up. "What is it?"

The boy opened his eyes, and then suddenly, Elliot was back at the mountain, hanging from the end of the rope, face-to-face with Megusen.

The mighty being's third eye closed. *"He is the boy."*

"He is the boy! He is the boy! He is the boy!" chanted the cloud creatures.

"They may ascend," said Megusen. He floated backward to his trunk and forced his massive body inside.

It was a tight squeeze, but once in, the wraiths locked it tight, picked it up, and carried the trunk away.

Elliot watched them vanish into the haze.

The boy, the old woman, and the octopus climbed their ropes and, once safely back on the ledge, they hugged each other. Elliot took a deep breath. The air was calm, and the path now clear, running upward to the snow-capped peaks of Mount Valkrius.

HANDSOME NED

Though the vision of the boy still lingered, Elliot hadn't the time to ponder who he was or what it all meant. They had reached the top of the mountain, and they had only one goal now: finding their gateway home.

Elliot looked up and saw the diagonal opening in the rock. It was just a short climb away. "We made it," he said.

"Not quite," said the octopus.

They started toward it, but just as soon as they did, a sound rose up in the distance that made them stop. It wasn't buzzing this time; it was something else. Like the creaking bones of an ancient beast. The octopus and Elliot ducked behind a boulder, but Yilba remained standing in place, staring out across the moonlit clouds.

"What are you doing?" Elliot whispered.

She refused to move. She just stood there, watching and listening, as the sounds grew louder. Elliot peered out from behind the rock, and saw something move into view from around the bend: a massive ship set ablaze in purple flames.

The ship from his vision.

It was towering and sinister, like a pirate ship, with rows of cannons protruding from its hull. The sounds were from the stretching rope and bending wood.

"What is it, Yilba?"

She kept her eyes locked on the vessel, watching as it moved toward them, its bow slicing through the cloud. It docked on the landing, and a rope ladder unfurled from the top deck, rolling down to plant itself on the ground. Yilba moved to Elliot, crouching down and looking him in the eyes. "This is where I say goodbye."

"What?" said Elliot, in shock. "Why?"

"Because ... I'm going on board that ship, and I don't expect to return."

"No! You can't. Besides, it's—it's on fire."

"Those are black-magic flames. They can't harm."

Elliot shook his head. "We're coming with you."

"No, you're not. It's too dangerous."

"Why? What's on that ship?"

Yilba paused. "Unfinished business."

"I don't understand."

"You're not meant to." She smiled at him affectionately. "Be thankful, Elliot. We both get our wishes, after all. You get to go home, while Granny Yilba gets to settle a score." She placed her hands on his shoulders. "Now, I've lived a good and long life. Some might say I've overstayed my welcome. Know that I face my fate willingly, and on my own terms. Shed no tears on my behalf."

Elliot's eyes welled with tears anyway. He hung his head. Yilba put her finger under his chin and lifted it back up again.

"Go find your gateway, and let it take you home," she said. "No looking back. Toot sweet."

The old woman turned and walked toward the ship. Elliot watched as she took hold of the rope ladder, climbed up through the fire, and hopped over the rail, disappearing from view.

"I'm going after her," he said.

"No, you're not," said the octopus.

"She risked her life for us. We owe her the same."

"We don't, Elliot. Listen to the logic of an octopus for once. She came here to settle a score; you heard her. She came here for herself. We don't owe her anything." He took a step forward. "Without a second thought, she led us through a world of demonic butterflies and up a mountain, surrounded by murderous cloud wraiths. How bad do you think it would have to be for her to say that going onboard that ship is too dangerous? Hmm? How bad?"

"Pretty bad?"

"Pretty bad!"

Elliot shook his head. "I just can't."

"Elliot, think of how far we've come. We're so close. Don't throw it all away now. Let's go home."

He wanted to. He wanted to more than anything. But try as he might, Elliot couldn't bring himself to abandon one of his friends. "I'm sorry. If I don't come back, just go. Don't wait for me."

The octopus stared at Elliot. Then he sighed and placed a tentacle on Elliot's shoulder. "This is not goodbye," he said. "You will make it."

Elliot nodded, then turned and bravely walked out from behind the rock. He stood before the ship. It was huge and menacing, seeming somehow alive. He took a deep breath, closed his eyes, and walked into the fire.

Purple flames burned all around him, but he could feel none of their heat. It was as if they weren't even there. Elliot clambered up the ladder and stopped, just before he reached the railing of the deck. There, he hesitated, gathering every ounce of courage he had left. Then slowly, he hoisted himself up.

Peering over the rail, Elliot saw the strangest thing he'd seen in a world full of strange things. There was a face embedded in the floor of the ship, a giant, fleshy face. It was brown and wrinkly, its contours melding into the wooden boards like a monstrous leather mask smeared across the deck. Its bulging eyes were staring up at a cauldron, hanging high above, that was dripping beads of phosphorescent purple liquid into its flame-filled mouth. The face gurgled like a baby, as an old man ambled across the deck, carrying with him a cage of butterflies—not the evil ones, the beautiful kind.

"Coming, Mother," said the man, putting the cage down to massage the crook of his back. His skin was pale, his eyes crystal blue, and he wore lavish silk clothing. But Elliot could sense that, under the layers of elegance, there was a deep weariness inside the man. He seemed tired, as though he'd performed this task a thousand times, and it was taking its toll.

From his hiding place, Elliot watched as a pair of wings appeared over the far side of the ship. It was a black butterfly, carrying the decapitated head of an animal from the end of its proboscis.

"Ah!" the man exclaimed, seeing the creature. "Well done, my child." He went over and took the head, then carried it to the face on the floor. "Open wide, Mother."

The face opened its mouth like a fiery furnace, and the man dropped the head in. The face's cheeks ballooned out, one at a time, back and forth, tossing the head around inside, and after a minute or so, it spat out a bleach-white skull.

The man caught it and carried it back to the waiting butterfly. "There," he said, as he tied the trophy to the demon's back. "Now, off you go and find us another!"

The butterfly turned and, with a horrendous screech, flew off into the darkness.

The ship, the face, the butterflies, the purple liquid, the old man, all of it made sense. The old man was Handsome Ned. Elliot was aboard the pirate ship Ned's mother had bought him when he was a child—the mother who was now a *part* of that ship. And the purple liquid dripping into her mouth was black magic, the stuff that turned the butterflies evil.

Elliot was at the source of all that plagued Lappanthia.

He knew now why Yilba hadn't wanted him to come aboard the ship. He also knew her secret, the one she'd been keeping all along. It had been right there, in her name.

Yilba.

Yilba was an anagram.

Yilba was Baily, Ned's ex. The one who'd run away.

THE DUEL

"Time for another batch," said Ned, picking up the cage of colourful butterflies, unlocking the little door, and shaking loose the insects. They spilled out into the mouth of the face on the floor, captured in a wash of purple flame, as Elliot looked on with astonishment.

Suddenly the face became agitated. "Mmmph! Mmmmph!" it called out grotesquely.

"What? What is it, Mother?"

Looking up, Elliot saw something that nearly made him cheer. It was Yilba, climbing the mast of the ship, with a sword between her teeth.

"BAILY?" Ned called out in disbelief. "Is that you?"

Yilba kept climbing.

"How did you find me, woman?" Ned spewed. All trace of his weariness disappeared now, as he raced over to a wall of swords, grabbed one, and scrambled up the mast at twice Yilba's speed. "How are you still alive?" he shouted.

Yilba reached the topsail yard, a horizontal beam attached to the mast. "Because I refuse to leave this world until it's rid of you!" she said.

The cauldron that was housing the black magic hung from a rope at the end of a boom. Yilba edged her way toward it, but Ned jumped onto the yard to stop her.

"Not another step!" he said, unsheathing his sword. Yilba turned to face him, and the two stared each other down. Ned looked bewildered. *"Oh, Baily."* His expression turned to one of disgust. "How you've aged."

"Have you not seen yourself, Ned? Or did you finally rid yourself of your thousand mirrors? Couldn't stand to see the truth of who you are?" She raised her sword.

"This is where it ends, Baily."

"For me, perhaps. For you ... most certainly." Yilba swung her blade, bringing it down forcefully. A clang of metal rang out in the night. She swung again and again, and judging from her poise, this was not her first sword fight. Ned responded with a succession of blows, pushing her back. Yilba ducked and dodged, and at one point grabbed hold of a rope, and swung around the mast to the other side. But Ned was immediately on her, bearing down with his sword, relentlessly hammering away.

Elliot watched as they duelled along the yard, high above the deck. Yilba seemed on the verge of slipping. One wrong step and Ned would have the upper hand—but Elliot wasn't about to let that happen. He decided to make his move. Jumping over the rail, he landed in plain view on the deck.

The face saw him and immediately let loose a horrible scream. Ned looked down and saw Elliot racing across the deck. "Oh, now who is *that?!*"

"No, Elliot! Go back," screamed Yilba.

But Elliot reached the row of swords and grabbed the smallest one he could find. Then he ran to the base of the mast and climbed up even faster than Ned.

"What did you do, Baily, call in your one-child army?" Ned scoffed.

When Elliot reached the topsail yard, he grabbed a rope and held on for dear life. It was a long way to the deck below.

The old man took a swipe, which Elliot managed to block just in time, but the impact nearly knocked him off the beam.

Suddenly, Ned froze, staring at Elliot in confusion. "*You,*" he said, as though recognizing him. "But ... how?"

Elliot swung his sword, and while it wasn't a powerful swing, it was enough to allow Yilba an attack from behind. Ned pivoted and put up his guard to block her. Then Elliot swiped again from behind, and Ned had to pivot back to block him. Then Yilba swiped, and Ned pivoted. Then Elliot swiped, and Ned pivoted. Then Yilba, then Elliot. Yilba, Elliot, Yilba, Elliot, again and again, making Ned spin back and forth over and over.

The old man began to panic. "Mother! How much longer?" he called down.

The face mumbled words only Ned could understand.

Ned swung back and forth, countering Yilba and Elliot—left–right–left–right–*clang–clang–clang*—sparks flying off the colliding blades. Elliot could feel Ned's blows becoming weaker. He was getting tired. All they had to do was keep him swinging until he had nothing left. Elliot felt a surge of hope.

Until Yilba's foot slipped.

She fell from the beam, grasping a rope and hanging helplessly in the air. Ned immediately grabbed Elliot and held him tight, pressing the tip of his blade against Elliot's neck.

"No!" howled Yilba.

"Drop your sword!" the old man screamed.

Elliot released his sword, letting it fall to the deck below, while Yilba manoeuvred herself back onto the beam.

"Surrender or I open the boy's neck like a stuck pig!" spewed Ned.

"Don't do it, Yilba!" cried Elliot.

"Shut up!" Ned pressed the blade into Elliot's neck, nearly breaking the skin.

"Stop!" said Yilba, dropping her sword.

"Yes. That's more like it," said Ned.

Yilba stood on the beam, defenceless, her long white hair billowing in the wind.

"*Yilba?*" said Ned. "That's what you've been calling yourself?" He shook his head, chuckling. "Oh, Baily. Baily, Baily, Baily. I've waited so many years for this moment.

Have you any idea what it's been like for me all this time? Wondering where you'd gone off to, and whether or not you were still alive. Rushing to the rails every time I heard the buzz of approaching wings, praying this time they'd bring you back to me." He laughed. "The head part, at least."

"You're sick, Ned. You're not well," Yilba said.

"Oh, that's rich, coming from you, after what you did to me. Do you remember what you did to me? Or did you cast it aside like everything else that mattered? Did you throw it on the trash heap next to my heart?"

"Let the boy go. He's not a part of this."

"But he is. And he needs to see you suffer the way I suffered."

"Ned, listen to—"

"NO!" Ned screamed, shaking with rage. "YOU listen to ME! This is your fault, you realize? Everything that's happened to this world is because of you! YOU made me do this! And now you will pay, and I will watch as you drown in an ocean of sorrow!" He looked down at the face on the floor. "Mother! On my command, release the butterflies directly into Baily's soul! EVERY! SINGLE! ONE!"

The face closed its eyes in preparation.

"No, please don't," said Elliot.

Ned pressed the blade further into Elliot's neck, making Elliot wince.

"Stop!" cried Yilba. "I'll do whatever you want, Ned—whatever you want. Just don't hurt the boy."

Ned stopped. "What ... did you say?"

"I'll do whatever you want."

"Whatever I want?"

"Yes. You have my word. Let him go."

Ned scoffed, then took a moment to consider, looking up at the sky. And as he did, Elliot saw the resignation in Yilba's eyes. She'd given up. It broke his heart.

"Mother?" Ned called down to the face on the floor. "Hold."

Elliot exhaled. Yilba had bought them more time. But how much?

In a quieter voice, Ned said, "All right. I want you to admit something."

Yilba paused. "What?" she asked.

"Admit ..." Ned swallowed. His mouth quivered. "Admit you love me."

Yilba stared at him, then, just for a moment, her gaze shifted, and returned to Ned. Ned didn't seem to notice this, but Elliot did. She'd seen something, and whatever it was changed the look in her eyes. They were no longer filled with surrender. They were filled with fire.

"Admit you do," Ned went on. "That you always have. That your heart sang for me the moment I first walked across that garden and took hold of your hand. Admit I am the most beautiful creature you've ever known."

"It's true," Yilba said.

Ned looked stunned, like he hadn't expected to hear that. Not in a million years. *"What?"*

"It's true," Yilba repeated. "You are the most beautiful creature I've ever known. I didn't realize it at first. I was young and naïve. I saw only what I wanted to see. But as time went on, and I grew wiser, I saw your true colours emerge. I saw your beauty in all its majesty. And it was overwhelming. It was too much for me. And so, I ran."

Ned staggered, overcome with emotion. It was as though a heavy weight had been lifted from his shoulders. "So ... it's true," he said, a tear falling from his eye. "You really mean it."

"I do," she said. But then added a definitive: *"If."*

Ned paused, tilting his head. "If?"

"If," she said again. "If beauty were the word to describe the scum between the devil's toes. If beauty were the label on the black hearts of soulless men—no, not men—cold, empty shells, deserving only of pity. Pity that they had never loved, and so never really lived a day. Pity that they were born innocent, but raised woeful and sad, gleaning joy from the suffering of others. Pity that they wasted a life of riches in pursuit of themselves, and left the world a darker place. Yes, Ned, if beauty were the word to describe those things, then absolutely. Absolutely, I admit it. I admit it wholeheartedly. No one comes close to your beauty, not in all the worlds across all the universes through infinity."

Ned began to shake. He turned a deep shade of red, looking like he was about to explode. He opened his mouth to shout, when a voice called from above—

"Up here!"

Ned looked up, and a stream of black ink shot into his eyes. "GAH!" he shrieked, letting Elliot go.

It was the octopus. He'd crept up the side of the mast,

skin camouflaged to match the pole, and positioned himself in striking distance.

Elliot screamed at the top of his lungs. "YAAAH!" And as Ned struggled to wipe the ink from his eyes, Elliot grabbed his sword.

"Throw it to me!" cried Yilba.

Elliot tossed her the sword.

"RELEASE THE BUTTERFLIES!" Ned screamed.

The face opened its mouth, letting loose the newly minted demons. Up they flew toward the yard.

Yilba ran to the end of the boom, swung the blade, and cut the tie that held the cauldron. Down it fell, past the swarm of rising black butterflies. She ran back to Elliot and the octopus, grabbed both of them, and threw them overboard, just as the butterflies entered her. Then she turned around and threw herself onto Ned, wrapping her arms around him and pulling him down, as they fell together in an embrace, toward the deck below.

Elliot and the octopus tumbled down the net to the ground, just as the cauldron crashed into the face, crushing it in an explosion of purple light.

The black-magic flames were now extinguished, and the ship sank into the clouds, slowly at first, then like a meteor plummeting downward to its destination.

And just like that, the ship, the face, Ned, Yilba, all of them were gone.

THE BOY

Elliot looked out at where the ship had stood mere moments ago. There was no trace of it now, save for the swirls of still-moving cloud left in its wake. He shut his eyes and turned away.

"She left this world a hero, Elliot, the way she was meant to," said the octopus.

And that was true, thought Elliot. She had. But that didn't make it any easier.

They sat in silence for a while, looking out at the expanse. Below, an ocean of cloud stretched clear to the horizon, while above, the shimmering spheres hung like a curtain of embers spread across the night sky.

How could such a thing happen? How could some-one exist in one moment, then be gone in the next? How could such a bright light be extinguished from the world forever? It didn't make sense. It wasn't right. But most of all, it was just very, very sad.

"We should go," the octopus said. "There's nothing we can do."

Yilba was gone. There was no changing that. She wouldn't have wanted them mourning her, anyhow. *Life's too short,* she would have said. *Toot sweet!*

Elliot and the octopus got up and shuffled their way toward the diagonal opening in the rock. They climbed to the base, and Elliot peered inside.

It was an enormous crevice. Ice clung to the walls, and there was a steady breeze blowing through, making a howling sound. It was haunting, but it also let Elliot know there must be an opening at the other end.

"Ready?" Elliot asked.

"Never. You know that," replied the octopus, clinging to the rock close behind him.

They clambered up and ventured in, and the deeper into the passage they went, the narrower it became. It got to be such a tight squeeze, that Elliot could barely fit through, and was so dark, he couldn't see at all. He had to fumble his way forward, feeling with his hands, and scraping his feet along the ground to make sure there weren't any sudden drop-offs.

It was truly scary. There could be anything waiting for them in the dark up ahead: butterflies, monsters. Or nothing at all. Elliot started having second thoughts. Maybe they should stop and turn back. But where would they go? They didn't have the energy or the resources to make it back to the ranch. And they certainly didn't have the wherewithal to avoid the butterflies along the way.

No. They had to keep going. They'd come too far to turn back now.

"You know something?" said the octopus.

"What?"

"This place looks better when you can't see it."

Elliot chuckled. Even in the worst moments, the octopus could still make him laugh (whether he meant to or not).

A faint hint of moonlight appeared on the wall up ahead. At first, Elliot wasn't sure, but soon it became clear they had reached the other end of the passage.

This was it.

The way home was just around the corner.

And when Elliot rounded that corner, he found himself in an enormous room. It was perfectly white and rectangular, with walls made of immaculately polished marble. The wall on the opposite side was missing—open entirely to the sky—and the room itself empty, but for a bed in the centre, a nightstand, and an alarm clock.

"What is this place?" said the octopus, looking around.

Elliot could see there was a lump underneath the bedcovers. "Someone's sleeping," he said. He was too far away to see clearly, but Elliot had a feeling he knew who it was. "Hello?" he called out. The person didn't answer. He called out again, this time louder. *"Hello!"* But again, the person remained quiet and still.

"Do you think they're dead?" said the octopus.

Elliot's heart beat faster. "I think I know who it is."

"Who?"

Elliot walked toward the sleeping person.

"What if it's a trap?" said the octopus.

But Elliot kept going. He stood beside the bed, looking down. And it was just as he'd thought. The person lying under the covers was the boy from his vision.

The octopus waddled over and joined him, and as soon as he saw the boy, he said, "Elliot, he's ... he's *you*."

Elliot shook his head. "No. It's the boy I saw when I looked into Megusen's eye."

"So, he's *not* you?"

Elliot shook his head again.

The octopus leaned in, studying the boy more closely. "Who is he, then?"

"I think ..." Elliot paused. "I think he's the boy who wakes the sun."

"You mean, the one Handsome Ned filled full of butterflies to stop the sun from rising?"

Elliot nodded. They looked back at the boy, and while he appeared peaceful on the outside, on the inside, Elliot knew the opposite must be true.

"How long do you think he's been like this?" Elliot said.

"A long time."

Elliot shook his head in disbelief. "How is he still alive?"

"He's an Immortal, remember? He can't die."

"Oh, that's awful." And it was. It was unimaginable. The boy had been lying there, drowning in sorrow, for years, unable to move beneath the weight of his own misery. "What kind of monster would do that? We need to help him." Elliot reached out and shook the boy's shoulder. "Wake up. Can you hear me? Wake up."

"That's not going to work," said the octopus.

Elliot stopped. "So, what do we do?"

"Well, we could try doing what I did with you. We could talk to him."

"About what?"

"Whatever makes him happy. Whatever he loves."

"But ..." Elliot looked at the boy, furrowing his brow. "That could be anything."

"Which is exactly why we need to get started."

Elliot leaned in closer. Looking at the boy was like looking at himself. It was surreal. Like an out-of-body experience. Elliot cleared his throat. "*Ahem.* Um ... I don't know if you can hear me, but I'm going to say a few things that might sound strange. That's only because I'm trying to remind you of what makes you happy, okay? So, if you remember, try to focus on whatever that is for as long as you can, and it'll make the butterflies go away. And once they do, you'll—"

"Elliot," the octopus said.

"Hm?"

"The cuttlefish's days in the ocean are few."

"What?"

"That means, hurry up."

"Okay." Elliot took a deep breath. He began. "Your home. Your family. Do you remember your family? Your mother? Your father? Sister? Brother? Do you have a pet? A cat or a dog? A hamster? Parakeet?" He looked for signs his words were getting through—any twitch or tremble, anything at all. But the boy remained perfectly still.

"Keep going," said the octopus.

"Candy," Elliot said. "Bags of candy. Cotton candy, jelly candy, rock candy. Candy canes, candy corns, candy sticks. Ice cream! Ice cream with hot fudge and sprinkles."

The octopus stepped forward. "Mackerel."

"Mackerel?"

"Why not? Everyone loves mackerel."

Elliot shook his head. "Kittens. Kittens and puppies and baby hedgehogs, rolling around in the grass."

"Warm currents."

"The ocean," said Elliot. "Laughter."

"Trampolines."

"Balloons."

"Rainbows."

"Toys." And so on, Elliot and the octopus listing all the joys they could think of.

"Swimming pools."

"Carnivals."

"Singing."

"Horseback riding."

"Kittenback riding."

"Dancing. Hey!" said Elliot.

"What?"

"Do that funny dance."

"What funny dance?"

"The one you did around the campfire."

The octopus looked puzzled. "That wasn't a funny dance."

"Sure it was," said Elliot.

"No, it wasn't. It was just dancing. Regular dancing."

"Okay, well, do it anyway. See if it works."

The octopus looked over at the boy. "But his eyes are closed."

Elliot shrugged. "Maybe he can still see. He's an Immortal, right?"

"Since when does being immortal mean you can see through your eyelids?"

"I'm just saying, maybe he has powers or something. Who knows? It's worth a try, right? Everything's worth a try. Please? Just one dance."

The octopus hemmed and hawed. "Fine. But it's not funny."

"No," Elliot said, playing along. "Not funny at all. Very serious."

The octopus looked for a spot to dance, and once he found one, he started stretching. He twisted from side to side, bent himself backwards, then wrapped his leg around his head like a rubber ballerina preparing to take the stage. Elliot was having a hard time keeping a straight face, and the octopus wasn't even dancing yet.

The mollusc bobbed up and down, kicked his legs in the air, and started strutting around the room, making funny noises: *"Cha! Tst-tst! Uh! Ya!"* He jumped and spun, shimmied and shook, boogied, tapped, turned and twisted. He flipped, flopped, flung, and flailed. He leapt into the air, landed on the floor, then popped back up and jiggled around the room like a bowl of jelly.

It took every ounce of Elliot's strength not to laugh.

Then came the squat thrusts.

The octopus crouched down and stuck (what passed for) his bum, up in the air, over and over again. *Squat! Thrust! Squat! Thrust! Squat! Thrust!* Elliot couldn't hold on any longer. He burst out laughing.

"Hey!" the octopus said, stopping his dance.

"Sorry!" said Elliot, howling uncontrollably. He fell back and rolled around on the floor, wrapping his arms around his belly and kicking his legs, laughing so hard, the veins in his neck bulged out.

"Are you done?" said the octopus.

He was not.

"How about now?"

Nope.

"You're going to suffocate yourself."

Elliot kept laughing until tears rolled down his cheeks. And when he was finally done, he sat up with great relief and said, "Oh. Thank you. I needed that."

"Glad I could be of service," said the octopus sarcastically. "Now, can we get back to business?"

"Okay," said Elliot, wiping his eyes. "How about jokes?"

"Jokes?"

"Yeah, do you know any?"

"Why?"

"I don't know, do you have a better ide—"

Suddenly, an alarm went off, and they both jumped from the shock.

"Shellen!" the octopus blurted.

It was the clock on the bedside table. It read 5:26 AM. Sunrise.

"Okay, that's it!" said the octopus, losing patience. "There's nothing more we can do. He's too far gone. Let's find our gateway and go."

"What do you mean? And just leave him like this?" said Elliot, motioning to the boy.

"Yes."

"We can't do that."

"Sure we can," said the octopus. "So where is it?"

"Where's what?"

"The gateway."

"How should I know?"

"Because you're the one who saw it in your vision."

"No, I didn't."

"Sure you did. You saw the mountain, the opening, the boy, the ship, everything. So where is it?"

"I have no idea. I didn't see any gateway. That was you. You said there'd be a gateway. What does a gateway even look like?"

"I don't know. You tell me," said the octopus.

"No, you tell me," said Elliot.

"No, you tell me."

"No, you tell me."

"You tell me!"

"You!"

"You!"

"YOU!"

"*YOOOOOOU!*" Elliot screamed at the top of his lungs. He was so exhausted. They both were. They had crossed a desert, climbed a mountain, duelled atop a pirate ship, and never once stopped to rest. They were so tired, they could barely think, let alone control their emotions.

"YOU said there'd be a gateway!" Elliot yelled. "YOU did! But there isn't! There's nothing! There never was, because you made it up! You just pulled it out of the air, and now we're stuck here at the top of a mountain, freezing to death, and IT'S ALL YOUR FAULT!"

The octopus hung his head. "Elliot, I'm ... I'm sorry. Octopuses are psychic creatures. You have to understand, we believe in—"

"I don't care!" Elliot shouted. He walked away, muttering to himself. "What was I thinking? Following an octopus. How could I be so stupid?" He stopped in the far corner of the room, wavered for a moment, then collapsed on the floor.

Elliot lay on his back, staring up at the ceiling. Never would he see his family again. Never would he sleep in his own bed, or pet his dog, or hug his sister. Never would he live the life he was meant to. He would die in Lappanthia, running from butterflies and infinite sorrow, and no one would ever know the difference.

Then Elliot's mind surrendered, and he drifted off.

GOOD MORNING

The alarm clock rang, startling Elliot out of a deep sleep. He sat up slowly, and looked at the numbers on the clock. It was 5:22 AM. Morning once again. He must have slept through an entire day and night. He stretched his arms and rubbed his shoulder, which ached from being pressed against the cold, hard floor all night.

"You're up," said a groggy voice from across the room. It was the octopus, peeling himself off the ground like a sticky wet blob. "Sunshine born upon the half-wave."

Elliot raised his eyebrows.

"Oh. That's just what we say in the morning," the octopus explained.

"Sunshine born ..."

"Upon the half-wave."

Elliot let the phrase sink in. It was oddly beautiful.

"That's nice," he said. And then it hit him. Suddenly and all at once, everything fell into place, right then and there.

"What is it?" the octopus asked.

"Sunshine," said Elliot.

"What about it?"

"That's what he loves. The boy."

The octopus paused for a moment. "Did we not say that?"

"I don't know."

The octopus paused again, then leapt up and ran over to the sleeping boy, shouting, "Sunshine! Think of sunshine! *Sunshiiine!*"

"No," said Elliot.

The octopus stopped. "What?"

"It's like you said, he's too far gone. Words aren't going to be enough."

"Okay? Well ... what's going to work?"

Elliot walked over to him. "He needs *actual* sunshine. To see and feel it."

At that, the octopus was silent.

"We need to wake the sun," Elliot clarified.

Neither of them spoke for several minutes. Then the

octopus said dryly, "Shall we put the moon to bed while we're at it?"

"Very funny. Do you want to hear what I have to say?"

"I don't know, Elliot. You're beginning to sound a lot like a sea urchin."

"Just hear me out."

"Fine."

Elliot walked over to the sleeping boy. "I think the visions I had came from him."

"Now you're definitely sounding like a sea urchin."

"No, really. Think about it. The cloud wraiths are there to protect the boy from the outside world, right? They're there to stop people from getting to him. But they let us through."

"They let Ned through."

"I don't think they did. I think Ned used black magic to *sneak* his way through. But the wraiths allowed us to pass when they realized I was the boy."

"But you're not the boy."

"Not exactly. But do you remember what Pete said about parallel universes? How each one has a different version of ourselves in it?"

"Vaguely."

Elliot walked back to the octopus and looked him in the eyes. "What if the boy is a different version of me? The one that exists in *this* universe."

Now the octopus looked intrigued.

"That's how he was able to send me his thoughts," Elliot continued, sounding surer by the minute. "The visions I had that led us here."

"Why, though? Why would he want you to come here, to this room?"

Elliot smiled. "So I could wake the sun in his place."

"Shellen's beak! They were calls for help!"

"Exactly," said Elliot, who then turned and started inspecting the walls, the ceiling, the floor.

"What are you doing?"

"There!" Elliot said, pointing to a dark patch on the floor near the edge of the room. He ran over to it.

"Careful," said the octopus, waddling after him.

There was a round seal, about the size of a manhole cover, embedded in the floor, engraved with a half-sun and half-moon—the same symbol Elliot had seen in his vision. "He showed that to me," Elliot said, his breath quickening.

"What is it?"

Elliot thought for a moment. "I think it might be where he stands when he wakes the sun."

They looked down at it in unison. Then the octopus glanced at Elliot nervously. "You're not going to stand on it, are you?"

"I think I have to," Elliot replied.

"What if something bad happens?"

"That's a chance we'll have to take." Elliot raised his foot.

"Wait!" cried the octopus, causing Elliot to freeze with his foot hovering in the air above the seal. "Think about this for a minute. We could go back to the ranch. I know it's far, but there's a chance we'd make it. They have food there, Elliot. *Food.* Lots of it. I saw cans in the kitchen—oysters, sardines. Imagine the meals we'd have. They have those giant kittens, and girl-humans your own age. And don't forget Tim! We could live there comfortably, while we figure out another way to get home. But if you step on that circle, there's no telling what might happen. You have no idea what events you might put into motion. You'd be risking everything."

Elliot thought about the All-Strawberry Store—the one from Yilba's story—imagining all the paths stretched out before him, leading in infinite directions. He remembered what she'd said about looking inward for the answer. So he did. And it was there.

"I want to go home more than anything," Elliot said. "But I know this is the reason I'm here. I know it in my heart."

"Elliot, think ab—"

"I'm sorry."

"NO!" cried the octopus.

Elliot stepped on the seal.

The octopus let out a scream, and covered his eyes with his tentacles.

They braced themselves and waited. Then they waited some more. But nothing happened. No flames rose from the ground, no bolts of lightning fell from the sky, no sparks, no fireworks. Nothing. Everything remained exactly as it was: just a quiet, empty room.

"Are we dead?" said the octopus, peering through his tentacles.

Why didn't anything happen? Elliot wondered.

Something had to happen. *Something.* But nothing did. Absolutely nothing. His heart sank like a stone, straight to the bottom of the ocean, and, for the first time in his journey, he felt completely, utterly hopeless. He hadn't a clue where to turn or what to do.

In that moment, Elliot gave up.

He reached out and took hold of the octopus's tentacle. It felt cold, like a little icicle in his hand. They stood together, facing the night sky, shivering against the wind. Elliot closed his eyes, and thought back over his life—as far back as he could recall. Then, quite unexpectedly, he felt a rush of warmth flood through him.

His name was Elliot Sebastian Wood. His mother was Janice, his father Stephen, and his sister Brooke. His dog was Poncho. He lived in a house on the shore of the Pacific Ocean. His first memory was of sitting on a beach, watching light sparkle off the backs of waves rolling in to rest upon the shore. He grew up on the ocean's beaches, and in its water. He loved the ocean as a home, as a friend—the ocean and everything in it, everything around it. Elliot felt this love, and from it sprang a path, unfurling into the future, as clear and deep as the oceans he would live to serve. That was the gift Lappanthia had given him. And it filled him with light.

A signal rang out from beneath the seal, travelling outward toward the sky—calling to something.

The octopus tugged Elliot's hand. "Look! LOOK!" he shouted.

A hint of purple graced the sky—just a hint at first, then more and more with each passing minute.

"It's happening!" the octopus yelled, jumping for joy. "It's happening! Ha-ha! Yes!"

The purple turned to pink and the pink to orange, then the darkness gave way to light, as the tip of a blazing fireball appeared above the horizon.

The sun.

"You did it! YOU DID IT!" screamed the octopus, wrapping his legs around Elliot. Sunlight poured in all around them, bathing the room in a golden hue.

Elliot looked at the boy. His mouth was twitching, his body shaking. "Get ready!" Elliot said.

The octopus turned away, and Elliot shielded his eyes. There was a burst of light, and when Elliot looked again, he was treated to the most incredible spectacle he'd ever seen. There were hundreds of butterflies erupting from the boy's chest, caught instantly in the sun's rays, and transformed back into their former selves—beautiful and vibrant, an explosion of colour moving through the room, like a swirling, splintered rainbow.

And in the midst of it all was the boy, waking from slumber.

Elliot and the octopus rushed over to help him. He was weak and could barely open his eyes.

"Good morning," Elliot said.

THANK YOU

"Thank you," said the boy, his voice weak and barely audible. *"How ... long?"*

"A long time," said Elliot, surprised the boy could talk at all, after everything he'd been through.

"Can you ... help me up?"

"Are you sure you're strong enough?"

The boy nodded. He slipped his legs out from under the sheets and they helped him stand. He wobbled a bit, then took a step, then another, and then several more. Then he stood still. "You may let go," he said, his voice a bit stronger now. They let go, and he teetered, but managed to steady himself. He looked around the room, taking a deep breath. "You have many questions, I'm sure," he said. "I will do my best to answer." His legs suddenly gave out and he nearly fell, but Elliot caught him just in time.

"Maybe you should answer them from the bed," Elliot said.

They helped him back, and he sat on the mattress. Looking at him, Elliot felt a deep connection with the boy, as though they were one and the same—two halves of a whole. "Are you … me?" Elliot asked. "I mean, are we the same, you and I?"

"In many ways," the boy said. And though he spoke with Elliot's voice, the manner in which he spoke was different. He sounded older and wiser. Which, being an immortal, no doubt he was. He could have been a thousand years old, for all Elliot knew. Ten thousand, even.

"Is that why I was brought here?" said Elliot. "Because we're the same?"

The boy nodded. "Barassas searched many years to find you. As shepherd of dreams, he alone can bridge the Ocean Illuna. The divide between our worlds. He was to bring you here. To this room. To me."

"But I escaped," said Elliot.

The boy nodded.

"Why didn't he tell me? That's why I ran. He wouldn't speak, and I got scared."

"Barassas hails from a time before language. He is incapable of speech." Suddenly, something caught the boy's eye, and Elliot turned to see what it was. A cloud wraith was approaching. "There is something you must see," said the boy.

The cloud docked at the edge of the room, hovering like a pontoon awaiting its passengers. Elliot and the octopus helped the boy over to it, and they all climbed onto the wraith's back. Together, they descended through the mist, keeping close to the mountainside. Elliot had no idea what to expect. He felt like nothing could surprise him anymore.

But he was wrong.

A person was lying on the rocky ledge—a woman, an elderly woman, dressed in a camouflage poncho.

"Granny Yilba!" Elliot screamed, his voice several octaves above normal.

She was surrounded by a group of wraiths that had obviously plucked her from the falling ship, and carried her to the safety of the ledge. There she lay—alive, but barely—withering in the shadow of the butterflies' mortal despair.

Elliot tried to recall what Yilba had told him days prior—what she'd need if such a thing were to happen. "We have to ..." He thought for a minute, and then he remembered. "We have to get her back to the cave! She needs to hear the sound of children's laughter!"

The boy summoned a wraith and, stepping onto its back, directed the others to place Yilba carefully on the cloud, along with Elliot and the octopus. "You will travel to Yilba's underground kingdom," said the boy. "There, Barassas will find you ... and take you home."

Home? Elliot wasn't sure he'd heard correctly. "What did you say?" he said.

"Barassas will find you and take you home," the boy repeated.

"As in ... Earth?" said Elliot, still not believing he'd heard right.

The boy nodded.

"The Earth we come from?"

He nodded again.

"Both of us?" said the octopus.

"Yes," said the boy.

It finally sank in: they were going home. Elliot's heart

nearly burst. "Thank you," he said, his eyes welling with tears.

"Yes, thank you! Thank you, thank you, thank you!" the octopus shouted, jumping up and down and laughing hysterically.

"It is Lappanthia that thanks *you*," said the boy. "Know that if you ever return, you will be welcomed as heroes by the Immortals themselves."

Every fibre of Elliot's being was ecstatic—*times ten.* But as the cloud began to drift away, and he watched the boy disappear into the mist, he also couldn't help but feel he was leaving a part of himself behind.

LAPPANTHIA

Elliot and the octopus flew across the sky on the back of a cloud, carrying with them their precious cargo: Yilba. Time was of the essence, as every minute could be her last.

The world looked very different by the light of day. Hills were spotted with vibrant colours; lakes and rivers crackled with light; and the trees stood taller, soaking in the sun after so many years spent in stasis. Everything was illuminated. Elliot didn't have to strain his eyes to see anymore. In fact, his eyes had become so used to the dark, he now had to squint, allowing his eyes to adjust. It was glorious, though. The world had awoken from slumber, and life had returned.

They flew back the way they had come, over the valley where Elliot was attacked by the butterfly. It had been a dark and foreboding place, then. Now it was lush and green, with a crystal blue river—the most beautiful valley Elliot had ever seen.

Over the dunes and across the desert they soared, until they came to the ranch, where he saw Pete and Virginia standing outside, watching their daughters tumble around on the ground with the giant kittens.

"Hey, guys! Up here!" Elliot called out, waving as he soared overhead.

"Elliot?" said Pete, looking up. "What the—"

"Can't stop! Enjoy the sunshine!"

"Well ... I'll be," said Pete, watching them go.

Elliot caught a glimpse of Tim, mending a fence on the edge of the property. The machine man was wearing Pete's sombrero, and it suited him well. It made Elliot smile.

Onward, over the wall of flowers, which stretched as far as the eye could see in both directions, even from two hundred feet in the air.

"If only we could bring some of those with us," said the octopus longingly. "Imagine the trampolines they'd make."

The wall was impressive, but it was nothing compared to the majesty of the Lappanthian forest, where fairy-tale villages sat on misty hilltops, overlooking orchards of silver apples and giant mushrooms.

Elliot could see people coming out of hiding, emerging from the dark to encounter a world transformed. Many were children who, having never seen the sun before, found themselves frightened and overwhelmed, having to be coaxed into it by their parents.

Over Haminia, the city where they'd met Tim. It was a web of winding boulevards and squares, connecting amphitheatres to concert halls, galleries to markets, inns to alehouses. Elliot imagined what it might be like when the people returned, when there was music playing in its streets, and exotic spices in the air.

"Incredible how far we travelled," said the octopus.

And it was. They'd covered a staggering distance, and on foot, no less. A miracle for a young boy and an old woman, let alone an invertebrate never meant to walk on land.

Over waterfalls and rivers, streams and cobblestone bridges, meadows and pastures and hills, until they came to a clearing, where they saw children dancing through the sun-dappled woods.

The wraith slowed to a halt and hovered in the air, and when the children caught sight of it, they all stopped what they were doing and gathered around, pointing up and hollering. As the wraith descended, they recognized Elliot and the octopus and started cheering, but when the children saw their beloved Granny Yilba lying motionless at their feet, they began to shriek with horror.

"*No!*" "*Granny!*" "*Is she dead?!*" they cried.

"No, she's alive!" Elliot shouted. "But we need to hurry! Get the others, quickly! She needs to hear the sound of your voices!"

The children organized into groups, and ran off as quickly as they could, disappearing into the hidden entrances of the mine to fetch the others.

"Elliot, how are we going to make them all laugh?" said the octopus.

Elliot gave the octopus a knowing look.

"Oh. Surely you don't mean—"

"Surely I do. You're about to give the performance of a lifetime."

"But Elliot, that won't work."

"Why not?"

"Because it's not funny."

"It *is* funny. It's very funny, and thank goodness, because it's going to save somebody's life."

"But—"

"Please," begged Elliot. "Do it for Granny Yilba."

"No," said the octopus defiantly. "I'll do it for you."

A clamour of voices rose up, as children came rushing out of the entrances, running across the clearing to surround them. Everyone gathered. It was time.

"Are you ready?" said Elliot.

"You know the answer," said the octopus begrudgingly. But he began stretching anyway.

"No stretching!" Elliot shouted. "Just go straight to dancing!"

The octopus skipped his stretches. He started bopping up and down on the cloud, twirling and bouncing, and a handful of children chuckled. But it wasn't enough. They needed more.

"Go for it! Give it your all!" yelled Elliot from the sidelines.

The octopus jumped, spun, and shimmied, kicking his legs as high as he could. Chuckles turned to laughter. The crowd was warming up.

"That's it! That's it! More!" shouted Elliot.

"This is humiliating."

"No, it's not! Keep going!"

The mollusc did the splits in midair, and when he landed, he launched into a series of rapid-fire moves: the corkscrew, the barrel roll, the limbo, the twist. He danced like his pants were on fire (if he had had pants), and the children ate it up. They laughed with abandon.

"Yes! YES!" Elliot screamed above the cacophony. He looked down to see if it was working, but Yilba remained still and motionless. No response at all.

Elliot knew what had to be done.

"Squat thrusts!" he yelled.

"What?" the octopus yelled back.

"Squat thrusts! *Do the squat thrusts!*" he screamed, demonstrating the move.

"Are you ser—"

"NOW!"

The octopus did the squat thrusts. He did them like they'd never been done before. He crouched down and stuck his bum in the air, over and over, until the crowd lost their minds. A deafening crescendo of laughter rose up like a symphony, then crashed down upon the old woman in a tidal wave of joy.

Elliot looked at Yilba. Her mouth was curling up at either end—*the beginnings of a smile!* It was working. *"MORE!"* Elliot screamed.

The octopus flung himself around—back and forth, back and forth, back and forth. He flung himself so vigorously, he torpedoed straight off the stage and into the audience, which only made them laugh louder.

Yilba was smiling fully now, and her body began to shake.

"GET READY!" Elliot yelled, but no one could hear him above the noise.

A burst of light made everyone turn away and shut their eyes, and when they opened them again, there were butterflies being released from Yilba's soul, spilling out into the light, and turning beautiful again. Everyone gasped as the colourful insects rose into the trees.

Yilba's eyes opened a crack. *"Am I in heaven?"* she said.

"You're home, Yilba," Elliot said. "And the sun is out."

The children showered the old woman with kisses and hugs, letting her know that heaven was as real as anything to be found in that moment.

GOOD NIGHT

The clearing was set with tables piled high with desserts. Carnival games were brought out and campfires were lit, turning the forest into a medieval fair. The octopus ate too much sugar, then spent the better part of the evening lying under a table, groaning. Yilba taught Elliot the cancan, and they danced like there was no tomorrow. Because, in a way, there would be no tomorrow. Not for Elliot and the octopus. Not in this world.

"I'm exhausted," the octopus said, looking over at the tents being set up for the kids. "Let's go to sleep."

"What about Barassas?" said Elliot. "Don't we have to wait for him?"

"The boy said he'd find us, remember? So, he can find us in one of those tents."

Elliot glanced over. They sure looked inviting.

"Okay," he said.

Yilba held out her arms and he collapsed into them, and she held him like a mother would hold her son. "You'll live a long, fulfilling life, Elliot. I've seen it in the stars." She kissed him on the forehead and said good night. And Elliot turned and walked away with the octopus, trying not to look back, doing his best not to cry.

When they reached one of the tents, they pulled the canvas flaps aside and peered in. There were two sleeping bags on the ground. They each got into their own bag, and Elliot lay as still as he could, listening to the sounds of the celebration winding down outside. And for the first time in a long time, he heard crickets. They had returned. The crickets, too, had come out of hiding. It was a welcome sound, soothing and familiar. "I don't think I've ever been so tired," he said with a yawn.

"Me, neither," said the octopus.

Suddenly, the chirping stopped, replaced by the sound of heavy footsteps. Someone was approaching— someone too big to be a child.

Elliot knew who it was.

The tent flaps opened, and a huge black figure stepped inside.

"GAH!" shouted the octopus.

"It's okay," said Elliot. "That's him—Barassas." It was the man in black. Only this time, Elliot wasn't scared. The Immortal moved like a lumbering bear into the corner and stood silently, head touching the ceiling, masked face looking down.

"I see why you ran," said the octopus.

"I swam, actually. Long story."

They stared at Barassas and Barassas stared at them. No one spoke. It was awkward.

"Is he just going to stand there like that? Why doesn't he tell us what to do?" said the octopus.

"He can't talk, remember?"

"Oh, right."

Elliot thought for a moment. "I think he's waiting for us to go to sleep," he said.

"Why?"

"Well, that's how we got here, right? Through a dream? Maybe that's how we get back. He is the shepherd of dreams, after all."

The octopus looked as impressed as any octopus could look. "You know what?"

"What?"

"You'd have made a fine octopus, Elliot."

Elliot smiled. "Thank you."

The octopus looked at the hulking figure in the corner. "How am I going to fall asleep with him staring at me like that?"

"What if I tell you a bedtime story?"

"What's a bedtime story?"

"Something we tell each other before we go to bed. Helps get your mind off things."

"Okay."

Elliot bunched up the sleeping bag under his head like a pillow and settled in. "Ready?"

"Mm-hmm."

"Once there was a boy who fell into another world. He met an octopus there, and they became fast friends. Together, they searched for a way to get home, journeying across a land filled with butterflies that steal your happiness. But with the help of an old lady, a machine man, and a singing cowboy, they made it through. And the boy saved the octopus, and the octopus saved the boy, and together, they brought light back to the world."

The octopus took a deep breath, as the crickets chirped outside in the moonlight—not the endless moonlight, the regular kind. "That was nice," he said quietly.

"I don't want to say goodbye," said Elliot.

"Me, neither. Why don't we do what fiddler rays do?"

"What do fiddler rays do?"

"They turn their backs, pass gas, and swim away screaming."

Elliot laughed. "We're not doing that."

"No, I guess not."

"What if we say good night, instead?" said Elliot.

"Good night?"

"That's what we say before bed."

"Oh. We say, join now the ocean inside."

"Join now ..."

"... the ocean inside."

Elliot's heart ached as he whispered, "Join now the ocean inside."

"Good night," the octopus whispered back.

Then they lay for a while, Elliot staring at his friend, wanting to hold on to the moment for as long as he could, not have it slip away like some dream that never was. But his mind began to drift, and soon he was wondering what time it was in his world, how long he'd been away, whether his family was worried, and if the glowing sphere forming around him was real or just a dream. Then his eyes closed, and the world around him was gone.

THE HOSPITAL

Beep. Beep. Beep. What was that sound? *Beep. Beep. Beep.* Where was it coming from? *Beep. Beep. Beep.* It was high-pitched and rhythmic. Annoying.

"Elliot?" said a voice, sounding a lot like his mother's.

He opened his eyes a little, and sure enough, there she was, his mother, sitting upright in a chair at the end of the bed—not his bed, a different one. Glancing down, he saw a needle embedded in his arm, and a plastic tube snaking its way up to an IV bag next to a machine—*the* machine—the one making all the beeping noises.

"Elliot!" his mother cried. She landed on him without warning, scooping him up in her arms, and squeezing him far too tight. "Oh, Elliot! Elliot, thank God!"

"Where ..." His voice was weak and raspy.

"You're in a hospital," she sobbed, holding his face and kissing him.

"*Why?*"

"Not now, sweetheart, just relax."

Relax? How could he? Relaxing was the last thing he wanted to do. He wanted to jump out of bed and tell his mother everything—about all the places he'd been, all the people he'd met, and all the adventures he'd had. He wanted to shout it from the rooftops.

But he was too weak. All he could muster was: "*Octopus.*"

"What, honey? What did you say?"

"*Octopus. Where is ... the octopus?*"

Suddenly, her expression dropped. She looked like a parent fearing the worst. "Honey," his mother said slowly, and with concern. "I'm going to get the doctor. She's going to come in and take a look at you, and make sure everything's okay. I'll be right back." Then she got up and ran out of the room.

This was the second time the world had turned upside down for Elliot, and it made him feel nauseous. He let his head sink back into the pillow and tried to relax, but all of a sudden, the doctor was there, shining a light into his eyes.

"Let's have a look, shall we?" she said, moving the light from side to side, up and down. "What year is this?" she asked, followed by, "What's your birthday?" and, "Where do you go to school?" He answered her questions as his mother sat on the sidelines watching, anxiously awaiting the verdict.

And when the doctor finally finished, she turned and declared ... "Looks good."

"*Oh!*" His mother exhaled, deflating into her chair.

The doctor went on to explain that she saw no signs of brain damage, expected Elliot to make a full recovery, and that he might be discharged within a couple of days. His mother nodded attentively, hand over her heart, but Elliot only half-listened, picking up bits and pieces here and there: he'd been unconscious for eight days, not in a coma, but something similar, a rare condition that impeded the brain's ability to trigger wakefulness. Whatever that meant.

Elliot wanted to correct the doctor. He wanted to tell her that he'd been wide awake the whole time, transported to another world in another universe, that it was not his imagination, that it was real. He knew the difference.

But he was too weak.

The doctor continued to speak, and his mother continued to listen, and a tear fell from Elliot's eye. Because all he could think about was the octopus, and whether or not his friend had made it home okay.

HOME

Elliot sat on his bed—his own bed, in his own room—staring out at the bay. The water was calm and still, and perfectly flat, like a sheet of glass reflecting the sky—like two skies, identical and facing one another. It had been two months since he'd woken up in the hospital. It was fall now, and school was open again. While the pandemic wasn't over, it was under control. Vaccines had allowed shops to reopen, people to visit one another, and the world to come out of hiding. And that was good. What was better, was that Elliot was home, and for that he couldn't be more grateful. He was truly happy.

But ...

He was also something else. Not sad. More like how he'd felt when Larry died—the little fish from the tidal pool behind his house. He felt like he'd lost something. Something he cared about deeply. Which, he had. He'd lost the friends he'd made in another world. And that feeling followed him around like a dark cloud. He couldn't seem to shake it, no matter how hard he tried. It was just there, everywhere he went, a constant feeling of ... loss. And he didn't know what to do about it.

A ball of fluff suddenly jumped onto his lap. It was Poncho, demanding immediate attention.

"Oh, hey, buddy," said Elliot.

Elliot hadn't spoken about Lappanthia yet. Except to Poncho. Poncho was different. Poncho didn't judge.

"Did I tell you I met another Pom there?" Elliot said. "He looked just like you. Not as cute, obviously, but he could talk. And you know what he said? *Tummy rub, please.* Just like that, with this funny little voice. *Tummy rub, please.* Is that what you would say?" Elliot looked into his dog's eyes, searching for any glimmer of understanding. "Are you trying to say something now?" How he wished he could hear Poncho's thoughts. How he wished he could hear him speak. But this was not Lappanthia, and those were not the rules.

"Oh, Poncho," Elliot sighed. "What am I gonna do?"

Poncho appeared to have no idea.

The sun was setting. Elliot placed his dog on the floor and went downstairs, through the kitchen, out the back door, and down to the edge of the water, where he stood looking out, as he'd done every evening since he'd been back. The ocean was soothing at this time of day, when the light was soft and the air was cool. He took a deep breath and let it out, trying to shake off the gloom as he stared at the ocean, and the sky, and the moon, and the stars ... and beyond.

Beyond.

"Hey," said a voice, snapping him out of it. It was Brooke, his sister.

"Hey," said Elliot listlessly, turning his heavy gaze back to the ocean.

Brooke stood for a moment, staring at her brother. "Okay, that's it," she said, crossing her arms.

"What?"

"You know what. Ever since you've been back you've been walking around like a zombie all day, with your head in the clouds, daydreaming, like you're not even here, like you're somewhere else. What's going on?"

"Nothing."

"Not nothing, Elliot. Something. And you're going to tell me, because I'm going to find out anyway, so you might as well just get it over with." She tapped her foot impatiently. "I can wait."

Elliot considered telling her: *I spent a week in another universe with a talking octopus.*

No. He couldn't say that.

I fell into a parallel universe and met my twin—an Immortal who wakes the sun.

He couldn't say that, either.

I saved a world called Lappanthia. While I was there, all I wanted to do was come home, and now that I'm home, all I want to do is see my friends again.

No. Just ... no.

He couldn't say anything. Not yet, at least. He wasn't ready. Neither was Brooke, who, even on a good day, still had a short fuse. So, he simply said, "I need more time," and left it at that.

Brooke unfolded her arms and turned to face the ocean. They stood side by side, staring out at the water,

wind lifting their hair. "We were so worried," she said, her voice cracking. "I was so scared you weren't coming back."

"So was I," said Elliot.

Then they hugged. And it was a deep, genuine hug. The kind where you never want to let go.

~~~

One night, Elliot had a dream. He was standing on the shore when he heard a splash. He turned around and saw little rings moving out across the water. Something was swimming there. Then a purplish-grey lump popped up above the surface.

Could it be?

The lump moved closer to shore, and the tip of a little head emerged—a slimy, gelatinous little head.

It was!

"Octopus!" Elliot cried.

The octopus leapt out of the water into Elliot's arms, and gave him a big, wet hug. They poured their hearts out to one another, recalling their adventures and laughing until the sun went down. It was beautiful. But it was also a dream.

He knew the difference.

~~~

In the evenings when the house was quiet, Elliot scoured the Internet for accounts of his condition—the mysterious "nocturniu syndrome." He searched websites and chat rooms, medical databases and blogs, but found little information. One article, called, "Sleeping Beauty with Rare Disorder Asleep for 70 Days," claimed the syndrome was caused by "a dysfunction in the hypothalamus," which, Elliot discovered, was a peanut-sized area of the brain, responsible for sleep, hunger, thirst, temperature, and a whole bunch of other things that seemed far too important for something so small to be responsible for. It was interesting, but it wasn't what he was after.

He was after an answer to the question that'd been bending his mind into pretzel shapes ever since he'd been back: was Lappanthia real? Had others who experienced the syndrome also travelled there?

He typed words into search engines: Haminia, illuna, Lappanthia, and so on, but always came up empty-handed. And with each passing day, he felt that answer slip further and further away, until one night ... he got an idea.

Rather than search for the needle in the haystack, let the needle search for him!

He would write a story about his adventures and post it on the Internet, and encourage visitors to leave their comments down below.

And he did just that.

He called it, "The Boy Who Woke the Sun," and after he posted it, comments began to appear. Most were positive. People seemed to like it. But again, that wasn't what he was looking for. He was looking for that one person who understood his story wasn't fiction.

That person was out there—he was sure of it—and it would only be a matter of time before they found him. It might take days, or months, or even years, but Elliot was willing to wait. Whatever it took, he would wait.

In the meantime, there would be soccer practice on Mondays, piano lessons on Thursdays, dinner with Grandpa on Fridays. There would be walks with Mom and Dad and Brooke and Poncho. There would be movie nights, nacho nights, and swimming in the ocean. But mostly, there would be the remainder of his eleventh year, which was filled with adventures of a different sort: a trip to Hawaii, scuba diving with manta rays, and most importantly, enrolling in a marine-science camp, where kids with similar interests discussed oceanography all day. They would continue their discussions after class, sparking ideas about how to save the oceans and the future.

"Kids can change the world if they try," Elliot told his new friends, leaving out the part that an octopus had told him that. But the thing was, he believed those words now. Kids can change the world. Because Elliot had changed a world—a world called Lappanthia. And if he could change that world, he could change this one, too. They all could. They had limitless paths unfolding all around them, as infinite as the worlds that lived and breathed, alive and waiting on the other side of a dreamy, upside-down ocean, possibilities illuminated by the shining light awakening within them all.

ACKNOWLEDGMENTS

To my wife, Jennifer, for everything. To Amelia for Granny Yilba, to Penelope for the octopus, and to both of you for understanding why Dada had to spend so much time on his computer. To Laura Bradbury for inspiring me to give it a go. To Bill and Sandra Evans for their support while I was starting out. To David Paetkau for the honest feedback. And to my editor, Beverley Brenna, and everyone at Red Deer Press, and Fitzhenry & Whiteside, for believing.

AUTHOR INTERVIEW

Another fantasy author, Madeleine L'Engle, said that "A book, too, can be a star ... a living fire to lighten the darkness, leading out into the expanding universe." In what ways did you conceive your story The Boy Who Woke the Sun to be this kind of living fire, to light the way for your audience?

That's a beautiful quote, and L'Engle's a brilliant writer. There are times I feel like I could write a book about writing this book. A lot went into it over a long period of time. When I first conceived it, I was going through a rather tumultuous period in my life, where I felt like I'd fallen into a parallel universe. Like there'd been a hiccup in space-time, and suddenly my life was on a completely different path than the one it was supposed to be on. I felt lost, and this book was born of that feeling. I found myself looking back on my life, contemplating the paths I'd chosen, or were chosen for me, or simply happened without choice, and how they all led to this point. And I pictured a boy trying to find his way through a dark, unfamiliar world. This book was about guiding him through it.

So, you're right, it's very much about lighting the way. And when Elliot wakes the sun at the end, that's his soul shining, because he's finally found his place in the universe. That's his path being illuminated. He realizes in that moment he has the power to affect the things that've been keeping him up at night, causing him anxiety—namely, environmental destruction and the existential threat it poses to life on Earth, to the future. Which is something kids are extremely concerned about, as they should be. I was, too, when I was young, and still am now. My hope with this book is that kids come away with a sense of empowerment, an understanding that anything's possible and they can affect change, even on a grand scale.

It appears that fantasy novels aren't as popular with publishers these days, compared to realistic fiction. What is the role of fantasy, do you think, for young readers? Was fantasy literature important to you, as a child? What are your favourite genres now, as an adult?

Yes, fantasy literature was hugely important to me as a child. It was my introduction to literature, really, and to film. My father read all the *Wizard of Oz* books to me, and Roald Dahl. He must have read *Charlie and the Chocolate Factory* a dozen times or more. *Jacob Two-Two Meets the Hooded Fang* and *The Secret World of Og* stand out as well. And *Star Wars* had a big impact. It was the first movie I ever saw. I read just about everything, but fantasy—be it for kids or non-kids—is still what I read most.

For me, fantasy is reality in dress-up. It takes complex, difficult themes, adds robots and aliens and faraway planets, and makes it more palatable, more approachable, especially for kids. Fantasy exaggerates, accentuates, and adds metaphor. In my book, for instance, the butterflies are these fantastical, demonic creatures with skulls tied to their backs, but they're also the pandemic. They're an airborne menace that flies around, causing suffering and death and driving the world into hiding. Kids might not get that parallel, but they'll no doubt feel it, which, in turn, can help them process emotions that might otherwise be too difficult to face head-on. Fantasy helps us understand ourselves and our world, while simultaneously providing an escape from it.

In his book The Art of Fiction, *John Gardner observes that there are really only two plots in fiction: a stranger rides into town, and a person goes on a journey. Do you think this is true? What made you craft an epic journey as the heart of* The Boy Who Woke the Sun?

I won't argue with Mr. Gardner, but I will say my story is definitely one of the two examples he gives. Why an epic journey? Because life is an epic journey, for everyone in their own way. *The Boy Who Woke the Sun* is about someone at the beginning of that journey, trying to figure out who he is and how he should move through it, which is pretty epic stuff.

Your book includes a lot of unique elements that work super well together. How did you come to include a trampoline-loving octopus?

That was a gift from my daughter, actually—Penelope. We used to play this game when I put her to bed, where we'd give each other three things—an animal, an object, and a place—and then use them to make up a story. "A story from your mouth," she'd call it, as opposed to from a book. One night, just before I started writing *The Boy Who Woke the Sun,* she gave me an octopus, a trampoline, and the ocean. So, I told her a story about an octopus who was swimming along the shore, when he saw a little girl jumping on a trampoline. The octopus was enthralled, so he waited for the girl and her family to fall asleep on the beach, then he sneaked out of the water, took the girl's boots, braided his tentacles together, and slipped his "legs" into them. Then he had the time of his life, jumping on the trampoline. And I thought, what a fun character. I wanted to see more of him, which is generally a sign you're onto something. And he ended up finding his way into the book—in a big way, obviously!

A week or so later, I was in need of a character who'd travel with Elliot and the octopus through Lappanthia, as their guide. I asked my other daughter, Amelia, for a name, and out of nowhere she said, Granny Yilba. So, just like that, Granny Yilba was born. It's funny how these things find you.

In your story, a butterfly's victim can be saved by giving the person something they love. In Granny Yilba's case, she requires children's laughter in order to recover. What would you say is your butterfly antidote?

A great question. For me, it's my family. As far back as I can remember, I wanted to be a dad. That was my guiding light, the place where everything was headed for me. I'd go so far as to say, my family's the only thing that makes complete sense to me in this world. And this idea of what makes people happy in the book—their "butterfly antidote" as you put it—is not always what they think it is. If someone were to say "money," for instance, that might actually mean safety to them, or security, or freedom, or self-worth, or a parent's affection. Often there's something deeper they're not seeing.

Although this is a serious story about how eleven-year-old Elliot overcomes many obstacles to find his way home, the story is also filled with humour. What role does humour play in a book such as this? How did you set out to create such funny scenes?

Humour's great for establishing connections. It can bond a reader to a character, or to the writer. One of the things I love most about the Harry Potter books is Rowling's voice. She's extremely funny, and you're instantly drawn in by that. You form a relationship with her voice and the way she describes things. Same as when you meet somebody new. If they make you laugh, you drop your guard, and it puts you at ease, lets you in. Humour can be great for throwing the reader off-balance, too. It can turn everything on its head. If things have been going along in a similar fashion for some time, dramatically speaking, a joke can reset everything, like a palate cleanser. It's critical that humour comes naturally, though, that it's never forced. Mostly I'm not aware of when I'm writing a funny scene, it just happens when it happens. It needs to be organic.

One of the strengths of your writing involves your ability to visually carry your audience through new landscapes. We swim in oceans, cross deserts, climb mountains, and encounter pirate ships, all presented in striking detail. How do you explain this cinematic ability to craft a story? Has it always been with you?

I was a filmmaker for twenty years, so that has something to do with it. But when I write, I try to visualize the scene first, and then describe what I'm seeing. And there's always this internal debate about whether or not to include something. I appreciate brevity, so I'm always looking for a few key details, the ones that will bring the scene to life for the reader most efficiently.

When Elliot enters the desert, for example, I realized what gave the truest sense of wonder about the place wasn't the plains of sand or the rolling dunes, but the sky, and just how enormous it was. When you stand in the middle of a desert, there aren't any trees or buildings blocking your view, so you can see the *entire* sky, which is really incredible. There also aren't any clouds or light pollution, so at night, the stars are so clear, you feel like you're floating out there in space along with them. Sometimes, the details that'll serve you best aren't the most obvious.

What advice do you have for young writers interested in polishing their craft?

Be persistent, be determined, be committed, and above all, be patient. Writing takes time. It took me five years to write this book, and a lifetime to work up to it. When I started *The Boy Who Woke the Sun,* I was forty-seven, and I still had a lot to learn, even though I'd spent decades writing screenplays. You need to study and practice. Read books about writing, take classes, watch videos—there are some great online master classes, enter contests, talk to other writers, consult with professionals to give you feedback, if you can. And read a lot. Not just good books, but bad ones, too. That's important, because you need to understand what not to do. Delve into it all deeply, and keep at it. You'll get better over time. It may not feel like it in the moment, but improving as a writer happens in slow motion. You pick things up gradually along the way, and they stick with you. No doubt you'll feel discouraged from time to time, but that's all part of the process. Feeling discouraged is just you pushing yourself to be better. You'll have moments where you feel like you have no business being a writer, that you can't write at all, etcetera, etcetera. But those are growing pains. Stick with it. It's hard work, but don't give up. If you want it badly enough, you'll get there. Every bit of time and energy you put into it gets you that much closer.

Thank you, A. T. Woodley, for following your dreams and creating this story!